ED

CW00456415

HITS

A CELEBRATION OF THE
CAPITAL'S MUSIC HISTORY

JIM BYERS, FIONA SHEPHERD,
ALISON STROAK & JONATHAN TREW

First published in Great Britain in 2022 by Polygon,
an imprint of Birlinn Ltd.

Birlinn Ltd
West Newington House
10 Newington Road
Edinburgh
EH9 1QS

www.polygonbooks.co.uk

1

ISBN 978 1 84697 532 5

British Library Cataloguing-in-Publication Data
A catalogue record for this book is available on request
from the British Library.

Design and typesetting by Edward Crossan and Alison Rae

Printed in Great Britain by Bell and Bain Ltd, Glasgow

CONTENTS

To all music lovers everywhere

Edinburgh is one of my favourite dreams. The Edinburgh Festival and the Tattoo in the castle. I always remember feeling very emotional about it, especially at the end where they put all the lights out and there's just one guy playing the bagpipes, lit by a lone spotlight.

– John Lennon

PREFACE

Edinburgh's Greatest Hits is a compilation of intriguing tales, curious facts and landmark moments that shine a light on the city's eclectic but often overlooked music history. The capital is acclaimed for its annual arts festivals yet music remains a lesser-known string to its cultural bow. It is not widely known, for example, that Edinburgh pioneered the live music scene in Scotland for a long period during the seventies, eighties and nineties before Glasgow developed its well-deserved reputation.

This book is a collaboration between Edinburgh Music Lovers and Edinburgh Music Tours – two organisations that promote the past, present and future of music in the Scottish capital – and we hope it provides a flavour of this beautiful, creative city.

At the time of writing in early 2022, the city's music scene, like those in many others, has been severely affected by the COVID-19 pandemic. It is not known how things will look when the smoke clears, but we hope the stories in here serve as a reminder of great music moments from days gone by and look to Edinburgh's bright future.

The stories have been selected for their entertainment or curiosity value. We make no claims to being comprehensive or unbiased. The key criterion for inclusion was that the stories were fun, noteworthy and highlighted Edinburgh's music credentials. We hope you enjoy it and look forward to seeing you on one of our tours or at one of our gigs.

Leith Theatre: a shining example of Edinburgh's past and future.

FOREWORD

They say you always remember your first time. For me, that means Barclay James Harvest at the Usher Hall. I was sixteen and didn't even own one of their albums. I think 'Mockingbird' was the only song of theirs I knew. But my mate Colin had gone over to Edinburgh from Cowdenbeath and come back with tickets. In my memory, the plan had been to go see another band – Argent maybe – but they were playing in Leith and we weren't sure how to get there from Waverley Station, so Barclay James Harvest it was.

It was tough being a music fan who lived in the sticks. A few groups played Dunfermline, but not many. Concerts in the capital, meantime, usually involved a skipped encore so you could run back to the station in time for the last train. Eventually, as our confidence grew, we started renting buses, which meant I got to see the likes of Jethro Tull, Genesis and Rick Wakeman – usually in the Odeon or the Usher Hall. Other venues would have to wait until I arrived as a student in the city in October 1978. At the end of Freshers' Week a band had been booked to play the refectory in Potterrow. That band were the Ramones. It was a far cry from Barclay James Harvest, and one for which I was not unthankful.

I soon got to know the scene in the likes of the Astoria, the Nite Club and Clouds and witnessed early and intimate (i.e. sweaty) performances by the likes of U2 and New Order. I remember Peter Hook playing some arcade game in the bar between sets, while the crowd of drinkers kept a respectful distance. At the Nite Club, Robert Fripp was able to move among the audience unmolested before his show. I think I was one of the few who recognised him.

Back at the University of Edinburgh refectory, the dining tables were cleared away so Pere Ubu could play (with The Human League in support), while another night saw John Peel bring his DJ set to the venue. I pressed a scribbled piece of paper into his hand asking him to wish me and my new band all the best on his Radio 1 show. He duly did, though the fact we didn't yet have a name meant it did us little good in the recognition stakes.

Fast-forward a few years and I was witnessing The Residents at the Queen's Hall and Tom Waits at the Playhouse (his favourite theatre in the UK apparently). And so it goes ... Your memories will be different; your favourite nights will be different. But as you flick through this book you will find a selection of brilliant moments from Edinburgh's musical heritage, stretching back to 'the kilted Elvis', the first British rock 'n' roller to appear on American TV, and including memorable cameo appearances by Bob Dylan and David Bowie among others.

The venues, the artists, the record shops – all are here to be feasted on. Well, I say 'all', but as the authors say in the preface, this is not meant to be a comprehensive (i.e. dry as dust) academic survey. Instead I would class it as a celebration of the city and its enduring love affair with music and musicians, venues and shops, one which will spark the remembrance of unique, high-octane experiences for all of us.

Ian Rankin

At 347 Leith Walk, Elvis Shakespeare have purveyed fine vinyl and literature since May 2005.

The legendary Vinyl Villains on Elm Row – named after a Police bootleg – have specialised in collectible vinyl since the early eighties.

Jackie Dennis compares dance moves with presenter Freddie Mills on the BBC's *Six-Five Special* in 1957.

LOCAL HEROES

JACKIE DENNIS

The Bay City Rollers are undoubtedly the most famous tartan-clad teenybop superstars to emerge from Edinburgh – in fact from anywhere – but they were not the first.

The city's first home-grown pop star, Jackie Dennis, who was born in Leith, was promoted as a kilted Elvis in 1958. 'The Kilted Choirboy', as he was known, couldn't quite compete with Elvis the Pelvis, as he stood only 4 feet 10 inches tall. It was said, somewhat unkindly, that his spiky red hair was bigger than his body.

However, this did not stop Jackie from scoring a Top Ten hit with 'La Dee Dah', one place ahead of Elvis's 'Jailhouse Rock' at number four. For a week, Jackie genuinely was bigger than Elvis.

With the proceeds from the song, Jackie bought himself a Ford Zodiac. This was a pretty sweet set of wheels at the time and Jackie personalised it not only with the number plate JD32 but also with an in-car record player. Very enviable, but surely a bit shoogly and not terribly practical.

More enduringly, he became the first British rock 'n' roll artist to make it onto US television when he appeared on Perry Como's *Kraft Music Hall* in October 1958. Later in life, Dennis worked as a carer in a nursing home. He passed away in 2020, but the Lilt with the Kilt will always be bigger than Elvis around these parts.

HAMISH HENDERSON

As organiser of the People's Festival Ceilidh in Edinburgh's Oddfellows Hall in 1951, Hamish Henderson played a pivotal part in revitalising the idea that Scotland's traditional music was something worth preserving, championing and nurturing so that it could continue to grow. Born in 1919, he died in 2002. His ideas continue to echo in the discussions about nationhood which Scotland has been having with itself more recently.

To his talents as a folklorist, poet and singer-songwriter, we can add his success as a political activist, left-wing thinker and leading light at the School of Scottish Studies at Edinburgh University. As well as Gaelic, he was fluent in several European languages. His mastery of German came in handy in pre-war Germany when, suspected of helping Jewish people escape the regime, he was pulled in for questioning by the Nazis. It is pleasing to think that they let him go because they couldn't believe a Scot could speak so many languages so fluently.

Despite being a pacifist, he had a distinguished war record and helped negotiate the terms of surrender of the Italian forces. His Second World War poetry is acknowledged as some of the best inspired by that conflict.

A staunch supporter of the anti-apartheid movement, he met Nelson Mandela when the South African visited Glasgow in 1993. Perhaps fittingly, Dr Hamish Henderson, to give him his full title, will be remembered for his song 'The Freedom Come-All-Ye', referred to by some as Scotland's unofficial national anthem.

We think he might chuckle at the fact that he is the only person to be honoured with a bust in both the National Museum of Scotland and Sandy Bell's folk bar.

Blairgowrie-born but a long-time Edinburgh resident, Hamish Henderson helped shape Scottish culture in the twentieth century and beyond.

The fabulously stylish McKinley sisters in 1963.

THE McKINLEYS

The McKinleys were one of the great unsung girl groups of Scotland. Born in Little France, Edinburgh, sibling duo Sheila and Jeanette McKinley cut their teeth on the same Hamburg scene as The Beatles (who joined their fan club) and went on to perform with The Rolling Stones, Donovan and The Hollies.

They released four singles in the mid-sixties, including the Phil Spector-ish 'Someone Cares For Me' and the groovy 'Sweet And Tender Romance', which featured on hip music TV show *Ready Steady Go!*

The sisters were dropped by their label after their singles failed to chart, and they moved back to Germany where they enjoyed some success separately – Sheila as a solo artist and Jeanette as one half of the duo Windows, who topped the German charts in 1972 with the chirpy Eurotrash tune 'How Do You Do'.

Sheila passed away in 2012, but in 2018 Jeanette came out of retirement to perform at a girl-group celebration concert at the Edinburgh International Festival.

THE INCREDIBLE STRING BAND

Edinburgh may have produced bigger music stars and more globally recognised names, but The Incredible String Band can comfortably be hailed as the most influential group to emerge from the city. Their inspired fusion of traditional western folk forms with Indian ragas and Moroccan music provided a countercultural shot in the arm to the city's flourishing folk scene in the mid-to-late sixties, and led to arguably greater appreciation in the US.

The group's initial stomping ground was the Crown Bar, a long-lost folk pub on Lothian Street in the Old Town, where Mike Heron – accountant by day, aspiring rock musician by night – was first seduced by the freewheeling experimental playing of Clive Palmer and Robin Williamson.

Heron was recruited as rhythm guitarist and, alongside Williamson, stepped up as a songwriter on ISB's pioneering albums *The Hangman's Beautiful Daughter* and *The 5000 Spirits Or The Layers Of The Onion*. The former was nominated for a Grammy, while the latter was cited as a favourite by both Paul McCartney and David Bowie. Both are still held up today as psychedelic folk masterpieces.

ISB were one of the first Scottish bands to tour extensively in the US. Their hippie credentials were sealed with an appearance at the Woodstock music festival in 1969. The band passed up their prime slot on Friday because of the danger of playing electric instruments on a rain-lashed open stage. Consequently, they missed their window to be filmed for the Woodstock documentary. On the plus side, they weren't electrocuted and lived to enjoy their legacy as Edinburgh's greatest cosmic crusaders.

Heron and Williamson reunited briefly in the late nineties. Both still record and perform (separately) but Heron has never forgotten their roots. 'Missing the Edinburgh scene of the sixties,' he says, 'is like missing the sixties.'

The ISB's Mike Heron and Robin Williamson
contemplate all things psychedelic.

BERT JANSCH

Neil Young described Bert Jansch as the Jimi Hendrix of the acoustic guitar and he wasn't the only esteemed rock star in awe of this Glasgow-born, Edinburgh-raised musician's virtuosity and creativity: Jansch's intricate yet fluid melodic style also influenced a younger generation of guitar heroes, including Johnny Marr of The Smiths, Graham Coxon of Blur and Suede's original six-string slinger Bernard Butler, who collaborated with Jansch in his later years.

His precocious talent was evident to folk veteran Archie Fisher when he tutored the teenage Jansch in the early sixties. By the end of their second guitar lesson, Jansch had picked up everything Fisher could teach him on the instrument; Fisher later remarked that Jansch had really only needed one lesson as the first tutorial had been more drinking session than music lesson.

The multi-talented Jansch installed himself as caretaker, guitar tutor *and* resident performer at much-missed Edinburgh folkie hangout, the Howff, but left the city in 1963 to busk around Europe. He relocated to London in the mid-sixties where he became a leading light of the British folk revival, both as a solo player and member of audacious folk fusion band Pentangle. After Jansch's death in 2011, Johnny Marr commented, 'There are people playing guitar who don't even realise they have been influenced by him.'

Jimmy Page of Led Zeppelin was obsessed with Jansch, hailing him as 'a real dream weaver'.

The Rollers take it easy in Edinburgh, February 1975, by which time they were one of the biggest-selling pop acts in the country.

BAY CITY ROLLERS

Some forty-odd years after the height of Rollermania, there are some who think that the Bay City Rollers were perhaps a little cheesy. Perhaps. They were also eye-wateringly successful and by far the biggest band to have come from Edinburgh with album sales of at least 125 million. By comparison, much vaunted boy band One Direction sold around 85 million. So shang-a-lang that, Harry Styles. That said, how much the Rollers made in royalties versus how much they *should* have made remains a controversial subject. Truly, the surest way to make money in the music industry is to be a lawyer.

An early incarnation of the band was known as The Saxons. Legend has it that they decided to find a new name by throwing darts at a map of America. The first dart hit Arkansas, but this was deemed deeply unsexy. The second arrow landed on Bay City, Michigan, and the rest is history.

At the height of their UK fame, in the mid-seventies, they played the Odeon cinema on Clerk Street three times. Their teenage fans were particularly enthusiastic during the 1975 gig – so much so that, after the gig, decoy vans were sent out to distract the girls while the band made a separate getaway in a police car.

Their clever use of tartan on their stage clothes gave the Bay City Rollers a unique identity, one which fans could easily and cheaply emulate – an important factor in the cash-strapped seventies. A pair of half-mast bell-bottoms with a tartan flash certainly did make a chap stand out from the crowd. Great onstage, less so when trying to slip away from a gig unnoticed.

PILOT

The Pilot story is a great example of why this book exists. Despite enjoying huge success in the seventies and the fact that its band members later played with some of the biggest acts in the world, Pilot aren't household names; nor are they widely known as an Edinburgh band.

Founding members David Paton and Billy Lyall played in early Bay City Rollers line-ups before striking out on their own. In 1972 the pair had bumped into each other outside the city's Central Library; later they started to make music together at Craighall Studios in Trinity, north Edinburgh. This meeting led to the formation of Pilot in 1973 and was later immortalised in their song 'The Library Door'.

Joined by drummer Stuart Tosh and guitarist Ian Bairnson, Pilot signed with EMI in 1974 and enjoyed a remarkable run, including two smash-hit singles and four albums in four years.

The 1974 single 'Magic' kicked things off. Reaching number eleven in the UK and breaking into the Top Five in the US, it went on to sell more than a million copies. The song's lyrics, which are about a 'day break', were inspired by Paton's experiences seeing the sunrises around the Blackford Hill area when he used to deliver milk.

Their 1975 single 'January' sealed the band's success, spending three weeks at number one in the UK and several weeks in the top spot in Australia.

Both hits were written in Paton's flat in Glen Street in the Tollcross area of the city.

Pilot appeared on *Top of the Pops* several times, and three more albums followed until, in 1977, the band split. However, each member enjoyed success playing with other artists. Notably, Paton and Bairnson played on Kate Bush's first two albums and also appeared on 'Mull Of Kintyre' by Paul McCartney's Wings; Paton toured extensively with Elton John; Tosh joined 10CC; Lyall worked with Dollar; and Bairnson played with Neil Diamond, Sting and Eric Clapton.

From The Album Of The Same Name was
Pilot's 1974 debut. Timeless pop.

THE EXPLOITED

Undoubtedly Edinburgh's most successful punk band, The Exploited proved prescient when they released their first studio album in 1981. Called *Punks Not Dead* – note the anarchist insouciance of the missing apostrophe – it railed against the idea that the rebellious genre had indeed shuffled off this mortal coil. The Exploited are still gigging, so perhaps they were onto something.

Early marketing campaigns by the band involved liberating newspapers, milk and rolls from yet-to-open newsagents. This swag was then left on the doorsteps of neighbours with notes saying the goods were a gift from The Exploited. Posterity fails to record what the shopkeepers thought about punk rock's answer to Robin Hood.

Four decades on, Wattie Buchan is the only member of the early eighties line-up to still be in the band. Riots, fights, bans, feuds with other bands and even a heart attack have done little to dull his ferocious stage presence. Now in his sixties and eligible for a bus pass in Edinburgh, Wattie continues to have an appetite for more exotic travels. The Exploited toured Russia, most of Europe and large swathes of North and South America as recently as 2019.

DAVY HENDERSON

Henderson has been making music since the late seventies, fronting idiosyncratic outfits such as The Nectarine No 9 and The Sexual Objects, and it is always worth keeping up with his manoeuvres. He played his first gig in punk band The Dirty Reds for the Edinburgh University Communist Society, then formed The Fire Engines, whose songs were as short as their overcoats were long.

Later, Henderson formed Win, whose chiming Scotpop anthem 'You've Got The Power' was used in a McEwan's Lager advert. In 2018 The Fire Engines reformed for the final time (allegedly). Ever the iconoclast, Henderson took to the stage of Leith Theatre in a silver anorak 'and not much else' according to a review in the *Herald*.

EXPLOITED

BEAT THE BASTARDS

An Exploited fan demonstrates why his career
in the diplomatic service never progressed.

BRUCE'S RECORDS

Even before he went on to manage Simple Minds from their early days to the height of their success, Bruce Findlay had secured his place as an Edinburgh music legend. In the late seventies, he ran Zoom Records, whose catalogue included The Valves' surf-rock gem 'Ain't No Surf In Portobello', but he was best known as the benevolent impresario behind the Bruce's Records chain, which serviced the needs of music obsessives across the Central Belt.

There were three branches of Bruce's Records in the city, including one on Princes Street and one on Shandwick Place at the West End, but it was the shop at 79 Rose Street that was the hangout hub for local musicians. Parading your purchases around town in one of Bruce's signature *I Found It At Bruce's* record bags was a badge of good taste.

Not to be outdone, other record shops in the city emblazoned their bags with pithy slogans. Phoenix Records on the High Street declared that they were 'Cheap'n'Nasty', and Listen Records on Frederick Street hailed themselves as 'the Aggressive Record Retailers' – though arguably not as aggressive as the peevish proprietor of the Ezy Records stall in Greyfriars Market. When asked if he stocked Faust, he was heard to exclaim, 'We sell music, no' f***ing noise!'

Hot Licks on Cockburn Street brazenly appropriated The Rolling Stones lips and tongue logo and were self-billed as 'almost Edinburgh's only record shop'. Situated in gobbing distance from the Wig & Pen pub, Hot Licks became a hangout for the city's aspiring punks and paved the way for a branch of indie stalwarts Avalanche Records further up the street.

Named after Michael Palin's *Ripping Yarns*, Ripping Records on South Bridge was the place to buy your gig tickets for forty-one glorious years until its dedicated owner, John Richardson, retired in 2016. Today, the city's record hunters are well served by the likes of Assai, VoxBox, Elvis Shakespeare and Underground Solu'shun.

Schoolkids from Stewart's Melville (boys) and Mary Erskine's (girls) bunking off outside Bruce's Records, 30 June 1980.

PETE IRVINE AND BARRY WRIGHT

Many have played their part in Edinburgh's music history, from the Waldman brothers, who were hugely influential in the sixties, to Bruce Findlay and George Duffin who were pivotal in the seventies.

In the seventies and eighties, it was Pete Irvine and Barry Wright who made Edinburgh the epicentre of live music in Scotland. Wright promoted Pink Floyd at the New Cavendish in 1968 and went on to stage numerous gigs (promoting as Cheap Thrills). In 1972, Irvine (promoting as Celtic Light) put on Dr John The Night Tripper and Hawkwind at the Eldorado Ballroom, a warehouse space in Leith that also hosted wrestling events. Later, Irvine staged Stockbridge Fair, Edinburgh's first open-air concert. In the late seventies, the pair formed Regular Music, and made Monday nights at Tiffany's one of the most important gig venues in the UK, booking gigs with a who's who of the day's biggest acts. In 1979, Regular staged Edinburgh and Scotland's first open-air music festival, The Big Day Out, at Ingliston showground, which featured Talking Heads. Irvine and Wright created Edinburgh's world-renowned Hogmanay events and ignited Glasgow's live music scene when Irvine persuaded Barrowland to reopen for Simple Minds in 1983. This former ballroom quickly established itself as Scotland's most famous rock venue, loved by performers and audiences alike.

FAST PRODUCT

Although Edinburgh had spawned a couple of short-lived labels, Waverley Records and Contemporary Records, in the sixties, Fast Product was the first independent to blaze a trail in the city and beyond, and the inspiration behind Tony Wilson launching Manchester's rather more enduring Factory Records.

Former architecture student Bob Last and his partner Hilary Morrison established the label in December 1977 with a loan of £400. Their flat at 2 Keir Street, overlooking Edinburgh College of Art, quickly became the party HQ for the city's punk and new-wave musicians, with the Tap o' Lauriston pub around the corner functioning as an unofficial annexe.

Describing their output as 'difficult fun' and 'mutant pop', Fast Product went on to release tracks by Edinburgh upstarts The Scars and Morrison's band The Flowers, while fellow agitators The Fire Engines recorded their cult classic singles 'Candy Skin' and 'Big Gold Dream' for sister imprint Pop:Aural.

However, Fast Product's earliest releases were by a trio of groups from the north of England – The Human League (who appealed for a deal by writing to Last on silver foil), post-punk icons Gang of Four and The Mekons, whose debut single 'Never Been In A Riot' took a playful swipe at The Clash's 'White Riot'. The Rough Trade record shop in London refused to stock this two-chord wonder because they considered it so incompetent. But influential music weekly *NME* felt otherwise, awarding it the prestigious Single of the Week accolade.

BOARDS OF CANADA

Subliminal messages in music, a studio in the Pentland Hills outside Edinburgh, several years between records, interviews by email and only a handful of live shows . . . numerous tales and mysteries swirl around this enigmatic electronic duo. What we do know is that they are brothers Marcus Eoin and Mike Sandison, that their 1998 album *Music Has The Rights To Children* is revered as an electronic music classic, and that they the went to school in Balerno and may now live somewhere in East Lothian.

TAM WHITE

Tam White was the nearly man of Edinburgh rock and pop. One of the most talented singers the city has ever produced, he struggled throughout his eclectic – some might say *eccentric* – career to find the right vehicle for his gravelly blues voice.

He grew up in a flat above the White Hart Inn on the Grassmarket, and won his first talent show, aged eleven, at the Ross Bandstand in Princes Street Gardens, though he achieved considerably greater exposure when he won a round of ITV's *New Faces* in 1974 and performed his single 'What In The World's Come Over You' on *Top of the Pops* the following year, delivering what is said to have been the first live vocal performance on the show.

White was a stalwart of Edinburgh's live music scene for over thirty years, playing in R&B bands such as the Boston Dexters, who styled themselves like gangsters and carried machine guns in tribute to Chicago's blues scene. White reformed the Dexters in the eighties and played regularly at the Preservation Hall on Victoria Street. When his music career stalled, he found success as an actor, taking cameo roles in *Taggart, EastEnders* and *River City*. He played the character of McGregor in *Braveheart* and provided the vocals for Robbie Coltrane's characters in John Byrne's TV drama *Tutti Frutti*.

SHIRLEY MANSON

The Potterrow student union was the location of an early sighting of a singer who would go on to become a global star. Shirley Manson played here with her first band, Goodbye Mr Mackenzie. While the Mackenzies never saw the success which many thought they deserved, Manson herself had the sort of success that few ever experience.

The Edinburgh-born performer had seemed destined for the stage from a young age and, as a child, had played parts in several musical and theatrical productions. When not on stage or, latterly, skipping school, the teenage Manson worked at Miss Selfridge on Hanover Street. Even from behind the make-up counter, her strong character made itself felt. One former customer recalled that 'Shirley Manson was the scariest shop assistant ever'.

Three American musicians, one of whom was Nirvana's producer, Butch Vig, certainly saw something in her. They invited her to join their nascent band and Garbage rapidly became one of the biggest rock outfits of the nineties. They sold millions of albums and, in 1999, were invited to headline a concert in Princes Street Gardens to mark the opening of the Scottish Parliament.

Manson became a fashion icon and a spokesperson for several causes, including mental health. She also became a member of a very exclusive club when she sang 'The World Is Not Enough', the James Bond theme song written by Garbage. She is one of only three Scottish women to have recorded a James Bond theme song: the others are Lulu, who performed 'The Man With The Golden Gun' and Sheena Easton, who sang 'For Your Eyes Only'.

Possibly one to remember the next time you're at a pub quiz.

SKIMO JOE MARY J BLIGE RYAN ADAMS

KEN KESEY
Life and Times
of the Acid King

Rolling Stone

SHIRLEY
MANSON'S
GUIDE TO
ROCK
"ou have to be a
"sychopath"

SYSTEM
OF A DOWN
Fist-Fighting
Freaks

CHEMICAL
BROTHERS
Kicked off Ibiza

NEW ORDER
o More Binge
rinking

CHUCK
BERRY
TURNS 75

PUDDLE
OF MUDD

GEORGE

PINK
FLOYD

ext

9 771320 061032

Wise words from Garbage's Shirley Manson on how to survive in rock.

MIKE SCOTT

While Waterboys frontman Mike Scott has lived in Ireland, London, New York and even Findhorn in north-east Scotland, Edinburgh plays a pivotal part in his story.

Born in the city in 1958, he went to George Heriot's primary school. He later alluded to the school in 'Edinburgh Castle', a song from his solo album *Bring 'Em All In*. As a nine-year-old, Scott recalls sitting upstairs on a bus and banging out a rhythm with his feet so hard that the driver pulled the bus over to tell him to stop.

Having moved to Ayr aged twelve, Scott returned to the capital in 1977 to study at Edinburgh University. With punk sweeping the nation, Scott embraced its DIY spirit. Interviewing bands visiting Edinburgh for his fanzine, *Jungleland*, he encountered Richard Hell, The Clash, The Boomtown Rats and others.

The Clash were a favourite; Scott met them at Hot Licks record shop on Cockburn Street, watched them play at Clouds and tracked the band down to the Old Waverley Hotel, where Mick Jones bought him a Coke.

Scott left university after a year and started his first band, Another Pretty Face, in 1978, while working in HMV at the St James Centre. After a move to London, APF split up and Scott embarked on a frenzy of writing that led him to creating The Waterboys in the early eighties.

Three albums followed in the space of two years, with the band going on to support U2 at Wembley in 1984 and releasing their most successful single, 'The Whole Of The Moon', in 1985 – covered by, among many others, Prince, The Killers and Frightened Rabbit.

In his autobiography, *Adventures of a Waterboy*, Scott recalls catching a bus on Princes Street and looking down into the gardens, wondering what it would be like to play the Ross Bandstand. In August 2015 he found out.

A recent Waterboys concert at a festival in Stradbally,
Ireland. Still writing, still recording, still touring . . .

THE REZILLOS

The Rezillos were (and still are) the most colourful characters on the Edinburgh punk scene – though they have always preferred the description 'new wave beat group', reflecting their gonzo garage rock 'n' roll sound.

Pre-dating the punk explosion, the group formed at Edinburgh College of Art, where they would recruit prospective members by going up to those with potential and saying, 'You look like a candidate for The Rezillos'. The successful appointees adopted stage names – singer Sheilagh Hynde became 'Fay Fife', because she was 'fae Fife' – and, in a show of true punk DIY spirit, they made their own stage clothes and props (including their own pet Dalek).

The Rezillos released one of Scotland's earliest independent singles, 'I Can't Stand My Baby', and went on to appear on *Top of the Pops* with their affectionate send-up song of the same name. However, in 1978 bassist William Mysterious succumbed to a 'flying saucer attack' and the group disbanded.

Fyfe and co-frontman Eugene Reynolds continued as The Revillos while founding member Jo Callis (aka Luke Warm) made it to the top of the pops in The Human League, co-writing 'Don't You Want Me Baby', one of the best-selling UK singles of all time.

The Rezillos reformed in 2001 and have been delighting audiences with their idea of what the sixties were like ever since.

The unique gonzo style of The Rezillos is seen here in the sleeve artwork of their 7-inch 'Cold Wars (Have Cooled Me Down)' from 1978.

THE PROCLAIMERS

Leith-born Craig and Charles Reid got nowhere in their early musical careers singing in the punk bands The Hippy Hasslers, Black Flag and Reasons for Emotion. Their fortunes improved rather dramatically, if not immediately, when they formed The Proclaimers in 1983. Their first gig was at a community centre in Cowgate, Edinburgh: it took place during a fundraising sale for the centre and the few dozen people at the event ignored the twins as they sang in the corner.

When they started out, they made no attempt to disguise their Scottish accents. Whether or not this was a political act, it flew in the face of convention. At that time, many Scottish bands with half an eye on a chart placing sang with a then-fashionable transatlantic twang. The Proclaimers were mocked in some quarters for singing in their natural accents, but, now one of Edinburgh's most successful musical exports, they are very much enjoying the last laugh.

Their songs were broadcast all over the world thanks to the film version of the jukebox musical *Sunshine on Leith*. Even Usain Bolt showed his appreciation when he warmed up for the 4x100m relay race at the 2014 Commonwealth Games in Glasgow by dancing to 'I'm Gonna Be (500 Miles)'.

A favourite at countless weddings, 'I'm Gonna Be (500 Miles)' is promoted by the Scottish Government as the optimum tempo for administering CPR or resuscitation. While the rest of the world resuscitates to the Bee Gees' 'Stayin' Alive', in Scotland we prefer to press 500 times. And indeed, 500 more if the patient is not responding. It all comes down to which tune you would like to soundtrack a near-death experience.

From playing the main stage at Glastonbury to rocking the Esplanade at Edinburgh Castle, The Proclaimers' career has had many highpoints but what are they most proud of? We would hazard a guess that it's 'Sunshine On Leith' being adopted as the defining terrace anthem for their beloved Hibernian Football Club.

Leith's most famous twins, The Proclaimers, have sold over 5 million albums worldwide. Their fans include Matt Lucas, James Corden, Kevin Rowland and David Tennant, who describes them as 'probably my favourite band of all time'.

YOUNG FATHERS

Edinburgh is home to one of the most endlessly creative and distinctive bands on the planet: Young Fathers. The utterly unique, uncategorisable melange of sounds created by Alloysious Massaquoi, Kayus Bankole and Graham 'G' Hastings can be traced back to 2002 and the dancefloor of an under-16s hip hop night at the city's Bongo Club. It was there that schoolfriends Massaquoi and Bankole met Hastings, and the trio have been on an incredible journey ever since. (Drummer Steven Morrison joins their live shows.)

First performing as 3Style, the trio explored their sound for several years in local venues such as the Venue, pitching themselves early on as a psychedelic hip hop boy band.

Success didn't happen overnight. It wasn't until 2008, when they were each turning twenty-one, that Massaquoi, Bankole and Hastings officially became Young Fathers.

After honing a more avant-garde and abrasive sound in local venues such as Sneaky Pete's, the band's career took off when their early compilation of tracks, *Tape One*, caught the ear of LA-based label Anticon. Follow-up *Tape Two* and 2013 single 'Low' paved the way for a career-changing year in 2014, which saw the band win the Scottish Album of the Year Award for *Tape Two* and the Mercury Prize for full-length debut *Dead*. Since then, the band have released two more critically acclaimed albums, toured the world, recorded with Massive Attack and had tracks featured in *T2 Trainspotting*, FIFA 2019 and one of Apple's global advertising campaigns.

But Edinburgh – or, specifically, Leith – remains their home. In 2018, sixteen years after meeting, Young Fathers performed a triumphant hometown show at Leith Theatre and they continue to record in their nearby basement studio.

A snapshot of Edinburgh musical history: Dave Grohl and Kurt Cobain play to an audience of tens in the Southern Bar. Nirvana's tour manager was Edinburgh native Alex MacLeod – brother of Murdo from The Joyriders who asked Nirvana to play that night.

WISH WE'D BEEN THERE

NIRVANA PLAY THE SOUTHERN BAR

In September 1991 Nirvana released their second album *Nevermind*. It catapulted the Seattle grunge band to global stardom and made their lead singer, Kurt Cobain, the unwilling spokesperson for a generation.

On Sunday 1 December 1991, just as the band were on the cusp of worldwide fame, they played an unexpected gig at the Southern Bar on Clerk Street. At the time, the Southern was a gloomy goth, punk and biker hangout – an obvious natural habitat for Nirvana. But, while they had yet to become global names, they were destined for much bigger things. 'Smells Like Teen Spirit', the lead single from *Nevermind*, had entered the UK Top 40 earlier that day.

Local band the Joyriders asked Nirvana if they would do a secret benefit gig for the Sick Kids Friends Foundation, a hospital charity. Nirvana had a night off from their scheduled tour and agreed. Word quickly went around town that some 'very, very special American guests' were to play the Southern.

By 7 p.m. the bar was rammed – by 9 p.m. the audience started having a reality check: would Nirvana *really* play the Southern? Many people decided not, and, by the time the band came through the door at around 10.30 p.m. there were only around twenty people still keeping the faith.

Bassist Krist Novoselic hung out at the bar while Kurt Cobain and Dave Grohl played an acoustic set of six songs. Cobain did so against doctors' orders: he had throat problems at the time and was also suffering from the stomach pain which plagued him throughout much of his short life.

Says Alan Edwards (who was there and took the pics to prove it): 'It really was quite surreal. It was all hearsay whether they might even be there. Dave Grohl was an absolute gentleman, and the music stripped down acoustically, well before MTV Unplugged, was just so raw and powerful. Nirvana's music has stood the test of time and is testament to the talent that this band possessed. To this day I am still so glad that I took my camera. It was all meant to be.'

After their set, the band lingered and chatted for a while. Dave was buying pints for the fans. Poor Kurt, still suffering, fancied a different tipple and asked Doug Johnstone – then a journalist and now a novelist – if he had any Benylin cough mixture.

In 1993, in the *NME*, Cobain remarked that Edinburgh was probably the only place in the world he would live other than his hometown Seattle.

THE BEATLES AT THE ABC

As Beatlemania swept the nation, Edinburgh was feeling decidedly left out of a touring schedule which had already taken in Elgin, Dingwall, Bridge of Allan and Kirkcaldy. A couple of local school-girls named Eileen Oliver and Pat Connor raised a petition to plead for the Fab Four to visit the capital – collecting 8,000 signatures from local businesses – only to be barred by their mums from queuing overnight for tickets.

But The Beatles became aware of the petition and the girls got to meet their idols at their two shows on 29 April 1964, where the group were pelted with their favourite sweets, Jelly Babies, and where 250 police formed a cordon to keep fans at bay. 'We love doing live shows,' said George Harrison, 'but, boy, those Jelly Babies.'

Screaming fans greet The Beatles at the ABC cinema on Lothian Road in October 1964. The band then headed to the Four Seasons Hotel in St Fillans for a couple of nights where they dined on steaks and attempted a bit of boating on Loch Earn before their Dundee concert.

PEOPLE'S FESTIVAL CEILIDH

Scotland's folk scene is in such rude health that it's hard to imagine a time when our indigenous music – from Lowland piping tunes to the bothy ballads of the northeast – felt more like a well-kept secret than a celebrated tradition. The People's Festival Ceilidh, staged in Edinburgh for four years in the early fifties, helped change that.

The People's Festival was established in 1951– according to its slogan 'by working people for working people' – to provide an accessible cultural complement to the more formal International Festival and Fringe Festival.

Scottish music had to be part of that celebration, so the poet, singer and folklorist Hamish Henderson was charged with organising the People's Festival Ceilidh. Its aim, he later wrote, was 'to present Scottish folk song as it should be sung', which meant songs that had been passed down sung by those who had grown up in the respective traditions.

Edinburgh audiences were more used to douce choral renditions of the old songs, and had never witnessed the likes of the Buckie fishwife Jessie Murray or Fyvie farmer John Strachan, or of future folk-singing legends Jimmy MacBeath and Jeannie Robertson, all of whom had been invited to perform at the ceilidh following a song-finding expedition by Henderson and the great American archivist Alan Lomax.

The inaugural People's Festival Ceilidh took place on 31 August 1951 in Oddfellows Hall on Forrest Road. The singing began around 7.30 p.m. and kept on going until the wee small hours. Henderson hailed the event as 'an absolutely unique thing in the cultural history of Edinburgh'. It inspired the foundation of many folk sessions around the city but its influence was also felt across Scotland, kick-starting the country's folk revival.

BOB DYLAN GOES ELECTRIC – EDINBURGH MIFFED

Bob Dylan played with his group, The Hawks, an early incarnation of The Band, at the ABC on Lothian Road on 20 May 1966. This was during the fateful period when Dylan was making the controversial leap from playing all-acoustic sets to playing electric guitar. Not everyone was a fan.

Three days earlier, at the Free Trade Hall in Manchester, Dylan had been subject to what is possibly the most famous heckle in rock 'n' roll history. As usual, the artist and band had played the first set of the gig acoustically – this was the Dylan the fans knew and loved, so everyone was happy.

For the second set, though, the band plugged in and started playing through their amps. The crowd was not pleased and, notoriously, someone shouted out that Dylan was a 'Judas'. Dylan shouted back, 'I don't believe you. You're a liar!' The band cranked up the volume and rock 'n' roll changed course for ever.

Three days later in Edinburgh, events took a broadly similar course. The first set was acoustic and the audience loved it. The second set was amplified and the audience did *not* love it. But they had a more passive-aggressive way than the Mancunians of showing their displeasure.

An Edinburgh crowd would be far too reserved to shout out 'Judas'. Instead, forewarned by the Manchester gig, they simply took out their harmonicas and tried to drown Dylan out.

GREEN DAY AT THE WEE RED BAR

At the time of writing, American punk band Green Day have sold some 85 million records, been awarded five Grammys, and have seen the stage adaptation of their *American Idiot* album become a global success.

The band were less of a big noise in December 1991, when they played the Wee Red Bar, the student union at Edinburgh College of Art. Depending on who you speak to, the audience that night ranged from ten people and a dog to a crowd of fifty. One account has the promoter saying they sold thirty-six tickets. Apparently, the band made the princely sum of £21. Mind you, tickets were only £3.50 for 'workers' and £3 for 'scroungers' according to a poster for the gig.

While the show may have been sparsely attended, the band still displayed a very punk-rock sensibility of all being in it together. One young shaver recalls how the band had a few drinks with their fans after the show. It was all very friendly. In fact, everyone got on so well that bassist Mike Dirnt kindly held the same fan's long hair back as he regurgitated the evening's snakebite.

LED ZEPPELIN AT THE KING'S THEATRE

The King's Theatre is a grand old venue best known for hosting an annual pantomime over the festive period; it rarely ever hosts concerts. But on 28 January 1973 an altogether different cast of characters took to the stage when Led Zeppelin played there on the second-last date of a 25-date UK tour (their longest ever UK tour). Tickets for the show, which cost a mere £1, sold out in two hours.

THE CLASH'S WHITE RIOT

Hailed as Scotland's punk epiphany, The Clash opened their White Riot tour in the Edinburgh Playhouse on 7 May 1977. The band enjoyed the gig so much that they played not one, not two, but three encores.

The audience were just as thrilled. In fact, several of them went on to form their own bands. Inspired by the DIY ethos of support bands such as The Slits and Subway Sect, Edwyn Collins returned to Glasgow and created Orange Juice while Edinburgh's Davey Henderson went on to form The Fire Engines.

David Bowie, 7 July 1973, bound for Paris the week after
he stopped giving concerts at the peak of his stardom.

FAMOUS RESIDENTS

DAVID BOWIE

The late, great David Bowie had a personal connection to Edinburgh: he and wife Angie lived here for a few months at the turn of the seventies. There are various properties around the city claiming to have hosted the Thin White Duke – Cumberland Street in the New Town, for example, and Dryden Place in Newington – but the address which keeps cropping up is a basement flat on Drummond Street.

It was owned by Lindsay Kemp, the mime artist and Bowie's mentor, and was apparently quite dingy: everyone slept on a shared mattress on the floor. The other lodgers included the dancer Jack Birkett and musician James MacDonald Reid. With assorted backgrounds that took in hard-scrabble beginnings, Romany roots, an abortive career in advertising modelling, a Gaelic-speaking family and – pass the smelling salts – a reputation for decadence, motley does not begin to cover just how disparate a crew they were.

While we presume the atmosphere was as convivial as it was cosy in the little flat, Bowie was seemingly not the most content of bunnies. In fact, one story has it that his time in Edinburgh might have seen him swapping his musical career for pantomime.

Bowie had released 'Space Oddity' in 1969. It had been a Top Ten hit but hadn't really made him a star. There were also suggestions that during this period he was questioning whether he actually had a future in music. Theatre was certainly a strong interest. Had Bowie chosen a career in dance or performance art instead of rock 'n' roll, it would not have seemed an unlikely option at this stage in his life.

Fast-forward to 2016 when Kemp gave an interview to the *Guardian* in which he claimed that he had encouraged Bowie to audition for *Puss in Boots* in Musselburgh, a small town six miles along the coast from Edinburgh. The assumption is that the pantomime was being staged in the town's Brunton Theatre. Apparently, Bowie was all for it but his management wanted £15 a week and the panto producers could only manage £10. In other words, a mere fiver made the difference between one future as the Thin White Duke and another, rather different life spent in provincial theatre.

Regrettably, there is a fly in the ointment of this story. Musselburgh's Brunton Theatre did not open until 1971 so Kemp's story should be taken with a pinch of salt. Kemp died in 2018, so we will never know the truth of the matter.

What is known for fact is that, while staying in Edinburgh, Bowie played a gig at Edinburgh College of Art. It was said to be the first time he had worn make-up onstage as a musician.

Musselburgh may never have seen his *Puss in Boots*, but Edinburgh did get to see an early incarnation of Ziggy Stardust.

MARK E. SMITH

Mark E. Smith, of Mancunian music legends The Fall, was pop's Mr Irascible, noted for his inimitable vocal delivery and inspired, lyrical juxtapositions.

It was rare to find Smith in a sunny mood, but 'Edinburgh Man', from the band's 1991 album *Shift-Work*, described by the Allmusic online database as 'surprisingly malice-free', is positively affectionate about the city he called home in the early nineties.

Smith hailed Edinburgh as 'the poor man's San Francisco' and his deadpan paean to Auld Reekie mentions walking the streets and bridges of the city at dawn. When he felt sentimental he'd visit the Black Watch monument on The Mound (his dad had served in the regiment) although he took against the Earl Haig statue at Edinburgh Castle.

In a 1994 Granada documentary, he described the Scotch Malt Whisky Society in Leith as his favourite place in the city, saying he felt accepted there. He was also partial to perusing the case files in the city's specialist science and law libraries. 'You could have a cig, and some fellows used to bring in hip flasks. Dead civilised,' he opined.

Smith had moved from Salford to lick his wounds after splitting with his wife Brix, now a noted fashionista, and lived in Leith for a while before moving to the New Town. Brix was back in the band in August 1994 when The Fall played a typically riotous gig in a marquee by the Acropolis on Calton Hill. Smith stormed offstage, and then back on to complete a shortened set, before the band had to make way for the next attraction: a late night show by stage hypnotist Peter Powers.

The Beta Band hang out on a video shoot. It was the nineties.

THE BETA BAND

Maverick music-makers The Beta Band are often touted as an 'Edinburgh band', which is *sort of* correct. Timelines are hazy, but the band's roots are in Fife, where Gordon Anderson and John Maclean met at school. The Edinburgh connection comes from the pair studying at Edinburgh College of Art where they met drummer Robin Jones and, later, fellow Fifer Steve Mason, who was then training to be a car mechanic.

The band became a fully formed entity in London after Mason and Maclean moved there, joined later by Jones and intermittently by Anderson. At a flat in Shepherd's Bush they started making music together and called themselves The Beta Band.

Visits to their old stomping ground bookended their career: the band played their first Scottish show in the Venue in 1997 and their last ever show at the Liquid Room in 2004.

STUART SUTCLIFFE AND JOHN LENNON

The Beatles also have personal connections to Edinburgh. Their original bass player, Stuart Sutcliffe, often referred to as 'the fifth Beatle', was born at the Simpson Memorial Maternity Pavilion on Lauriston Place in 1940. Tragically, he died of a brain haemorrhage at the age of twenty-one, having left the band the year before.

John Lennon's Aunt Mater lived in Murrayfield, and, as a boy, he would visit her Ormidale Terrace home for a week every summer. Presumably these were rather wet summers as he wrote 'Rain', the B-side to 'Paperback Writer', while in the city.

The teenage Lennon loved hanging out with his older cousin Stan Parkes, often at the Roxy Cinema on Gorgie Road. The cupboard under the stairs was another favourite retreat, though this is not some foreshadowing of Harry Potter – it was simply where the telephone was located.

Lennon would travel up to Edinburgh by bus, on one occasion annoying his fellow passengers with his incessant chirruping on a cheap harmonica. The driver heard it differently though and gifted him a more sophisticated moothie which had been left on the bus. Lennon put it to good use on the recordings of 'Love Me Do' and 'Please Please Me', and later played it at The Beatles' ABC gig in 1964, before shunning the band's hotel to crash at Stan's house in Bryce Crescent.

Post-Beatles, Lennon returned to Edinburgh with Yoko Ono, his son Julian and Ono's daughter Kyoko. Occasionally signing his letters 'Jock Lennon', he said he 'always felt free in Scotland' and expressed regret at not buying his aunt's Murrayfield house which was said to have influenced 'In My Life'.

NICO

The life story of imperious Velvet Underground chanteuse Nico, whose deadpan alto graced some of their most haunting songs, is a sad and slightly slippery affair. One of its least documented episodes is the brief interlude in the early eighties which she spent living on St Stephen Street in Stockbridge with her then partner, Robert King.

King, now based in Lyon, was frontman of one of Edinburgh's most iconoclastic bands The Scars, provocative punk outsiders who dared to flirt with glam rock, man make-up and improv indulgence. They were Fast Product's hometown signings, lauded for their debut single, 'Adult/ery/Horrorshow', yet chastised for their only album *Author! Author!* (now a classic) before King left the band and the charismatic couple drifted off to Manchester.

Nico did perform live before leaving Edinburgh, delivering what *The List* later described as a 'seemingly endless set', including a rambling version of 'Deutschland Über Alles', at the Nite Club above the Playhouse.

Her tenure in Auld Reekie may have been transitory but she must have put her stamp on the city. When her former VU compadres opened their 1993 reunion tour in Edinburgh, they were heckled with the declaration that 'this is Nico's town'.

Jazz (and chess) virtuoso Dizzy Gillespie in 1978.

THE BIZARRE

DIZZY GILLESPIE

In the late seventies, the jazz saxophonist and club owner Ronnie Scott hired the Nite Club above the Playhouse for a run of shows during the Fringe. The star attraction was Dizzy Gillespie, who was as great a chess player as he was a jazz trumpeter.

Apparently, he set up his board in the corner of the dressing room and took on all comers. No one could lay a finger on him and opponent after opponent was swiftly defeated.

The reason for his success? Gillespie would always invite his foe to take the white pieces and play first. While his competitor was contemplating his move, the trumpeter would take out his pipe and pack the bowl with his favourite herb. Gillespie would spark up, enjoy a couple of deep draws and then pass the pipe to the other player.

Whatever was in the pipe, it had a disorienting effect. After a couple of puffs on the pipe, few could think straight, never mind strategically, and Gillespie would rapidly achieve checkmate. One musician who knew Gillespie described his dressing room as always smelling like a Mexican forest fire.

QUOI?

In 1987, a year before her surprise Eurovision Song Contest victory, a 19-year-old Céline Dion came to Edinburgh to shoot a video for her single 'Lolita (Trop Jeune Pour Aimer)'. Trilling in her native French, Céline strides around the city in, variously, a cropped bronze leather bomber jacket and stonewashed denim. After boarding an LRT bus, she takes in the sights and then narrowly avoids getting run down by the traffic at the east end of Princes Street. A snapshot of shoe shop Dolcis will raise a nostalgic smile. *C'est fantastique!*

ANEKA

One of Scotland's unlikeliest pop stars, Aneka hit the top of the charts in August 1981, dressed in a kimono and enquiring as to the whereabouts of her Japanese boy. The singer under the angular black wig was Edinburgh-born Mary Sandeman, an established Gaelic singer who had won the Gold Medal at the 1976 Royal National Mòd but fancied a stab at the pop charts.

Her pop moniker was picked out of the Edinburgh telephone directory for its perceived exoticism and the hastily produced 'Japanese Boy' was released on Berlin's Hansa label, the home of Boney M.

Sandeman was performing at the Edinburgh Festival on the day she discovered her novelty ditty had gone to number one in the UK Singles Chart.

An album was released but subsequent singles flopped, securing Aneka time-honoured one-hit-wonder status.

'Japanese Boy' was a hit throughout Europe and North America but never in Japan where, according to Sandeman in a 2011 interview with the *Daily Record*, it was considered 'too Chinese'.

PROSTHETIC LIMBS

Among the many items of lost property found in Sandy Bell's folk bar was a set of prosthetic limbs adorned with a Post-It note reading 'Send me to Auchtermuchty'. The shaggy-dog-tale aspects of the story mean it is beyond the ambition of this modest book to recount in full. Needless to say, drink had been taken.

FAUST

Arguably the most experimental Krautrock band, Faust are known for their unconventional gigs. Their uncompromising approach to their art has led to them drilling through stages, playing gigs naked and using concrete mixers to make their music. They also have a penchant for pyrotechnics.

Depending on your point of view, this trait proved disastrous or dazzling when they played a rare gig at the Jaffa Cake on King's Stables Road in 1997. Part of the Flux Festival, the gig took an unexpected turn when the band set off a flare. Billowing smoke led to the evacuation of the VIP gallery, and Faust's reputation for anarchy as entertainment was further entrenched.

JIMMY THE PHANTOM DRUMMER

It is said that Edinburgh Castle is haunted by a headless drummer boy who manifests when the castle is under attack. In the seventies, the music venues of Edinburgh had their own rather more corporeal 'phantom' drummer, Jimmy, who would turn up at gigs with his own drum and sticks, play along with bands from the audience and occasionally be rewarded with his own encore.

His favourite haunting ground was Eric Brown's on Dalry Road. This live music bar was owned by professional golfer Eric Brown and hosted early gigs by The Exploited, The Associates and The Thompson Twins. It was thought to be a bad omen if Jimmy wasn't drumming along at your show.

THINGS THAT GO BUMP IN THE NIGHT

The Edinburgh Playhouse is one of the UK's many haunted theatres. From the 1950s, staff members have reported seeing a man dressed in grey on the sixth level of the theatre. His appearances are accompanied by a blast of cold air. His identity is unknown, but 'Albert' is thought to be the ghost of a stage hand or night-watchman who killed himself in the building. As recently as 1997, prior to a Commonwealth Heads of Government summit meeting, sniffer dogs were called in to search the venue for bombs. But the dogs, allegedly, refused to enter Level Six.

Greek-born Hamburg resident Vicky Leandros wins the Eurovision Song
Contest for Luxembourg in March 1972. She was still recording and touring a
few years ago after a spell as a town councillor in the Greek town of Piraeus.

DID YOU KNOW?

EUROVISION

Edinburgh is the only Scottish city to have hosted the much-loved cheese fest that is the Eurovision Song Contest. Monaco won the competition in 1971 but, in contravention of established custom, failed to muster a suitable venue for the next year's bash. Edinburgh stepped into the breach and, in 1972, the competition was held in the Usher Hall.

While the performances took place in the Lothian Road venue, the judges were sequestered in Edinburgh Castle, where they watched the competitors on television. They were kept in isolation as the organisers were afraid that malign forces would try to nobble the jury.

One version of history has it that the Spanish dictator Franco had done just that a few years earlier and robbed Cliff Richard of victory in the dastardly process. Allegedly, the jury was rigged so that Spain won and would host the competition the following year. If true, it would be one of the dictator's less toxic crimes.

Of course, 1972 was back in the days when Britain was able to enter the competition without fear of nul points and The New Seekers, featuring Scottish singer Eve Graham, came a respectable second with 'Beg, Steal Or Borrow' to eventual winner Vicky Leandros of Luxembourg.

MTV MAKES A SPLASH IN LEITH

When the MTV Europe Music Awards landed in Leith in November 2003, it was a big moment for Edinburgh. With Beyoncé, Missy Elliott and Justin Timberlake among the stars present inside a gigantic temporary tented arena at Ocean Terminal, an estimated one billion people in twenty-eight countries around the globe watched the show.

Winner of Best Male, Best Pop and Best Album, Timberlake commented that it was his first time in Scotland and 'you don't get nicer than you people'. Aw, shucks. At one point, host Vin Diesel, resplendent in black leather kilt, sang 'Flower Of Scotland' to everyone's delight.

The event was a huge success, boosting the local economy and strengthening Edinburgh's position on the music map, yet plans to host similar large-scale events in a permanent venue came to nothing – a huge missed opportunity.

JOAN BAEZ'S MUM

Joan Bridge Baez, mother of the esteemed folk singer Joan Baez, originally hailed from Edinburgh (she was born here in 1913), but her family emigrated to the US. It was there that she met Albert Baez at a high school dance in New Jersey.

'Big Joan', as she became known, was a committed pacifist and, in 1967, was arrested along with 'Wee Joan' at a Vietnam War protest in Oakland, CA.

She died in 2013, just a few days after her hundredth birthday. Her parting words to her family were, 'Don't grieve . . . make the bottles pop. You know I love champagne almost as much as I love you!'

BUSKING IT

No tourist trip to Edinburgh is complete without the obligatory photo opportunity with the bagpiping busker on the Royal Mile. But those in the right place at the right time might just have spotted a well kent face . . .

In May 1985, The Clash embarked on a busking tour of the UK, performing impromptu pop-up sets in a handful of venues in each city they visited. Prior to their guerilla gig at La Sorbonne on the Cowgate, frontman Joe Strummer took it outside, where he was spotted busking 'for beer money' on Princes Street and at the St James Centre.

Warren Ellis is known today as Nick Cave's trusty right-hand man in The Bad Seeds, wielding his violin like a lead guitar. But back in 1988, before he had even joined a band, Ellis travelled around Europe, learning Scottish and Irish fiddle tunes as he went. Arriving in Edinburgh, he cut his teeth and probably broke a few strings busking every day in what he remembers as 'that really f***ing cold train station just off the Golden Mile'. We suspect he means Waverley Station and the Royal Mile.

Busking remains a tough gig – but during the COVID pandemic, it was also the only gig. In October 2020, Princes Street busker Matt Grant saw his livelihood slip away when he was accosted by a drunk woman, who swiped his guitar and proceeded to smash it to bits on the pavement. Over in Nashville, White Stripes frontman Jack White read of his travails, charged his manager with tracking down the unlucky street musician and paid for the guitar of Grant's dreams. Cue another al fresco rendition of 'Seven Nation Army', this one on a £3,600 Fender Stratocaster.

Well, hello, laydeez . . . Judge Dread worked as a nightclub bouncer, DJ and debt collector for Trojan Records before he started to make his own music.

JAMAICAN REGGAE SPICES UP THE FESTIVAL

Audiences at the Edinburgh International Festival are accustomed to expecting the unexpected, but they encountered a considerable curveball in 1973 when Bruce Findlay of local record shop Bruce's Records staged a concert at the Empire Theatre showcasing some of the primo London-based reggae artists signed to Jamaica's legendary Trojan Records. The show was part of Findlay's Edinburgh Pop Festival, one of the city's first festivals, which ran for almost two weeks and featured shows by Procol Harum and Can. It was recorded by *The Old Grey Whistle Test*, but wasn't broadcast at the time. In 2011, as part of BBC Four's *Reggae Britannia* series, the footage of ska veterans the Pioneers, Nicky Thomas, Winston Groovy and Dennis Alcapone performing to a politely appreciative audience resurfaced.

Tickets for the event cost 25p and the show was compered by English MC and musician Judge Dread (born Alexander Minto Hughes), a former Rolling Stones bodyguard and professional wrestler. In the seventies, his innuendo-laced singles such as 'Big Six' and 'Big Ten' racked up more UK sales than any other reggae artist apart from Bob Marley, and he holds the Guinness World Record for most songs banned by the BBC.

PUNK CLASSIC WRITTEN IN EDINBURGH

Several sources verify the tale that the Buzzcocks wrote their punk-pop classic 'Ever Fallen In Love (With Someone You Shouldn't've)' while on tour in the city. The story goes that the band were watching *Guys and Dolls* in a guesthouse near Leith Walk when Pete Shelley's ears pricked up at the line: 'Wait till you fall for somebody.'

The next day, 5 November 1977, one of the band had to post a parcel at the old post office on Waterloo Place. The line still in his head, Shelley wrote the lyrics while waiting in the band's Transit van.

SANDY BELL'S

Arguably Edinburgh's best-loved folk music bar, the Sandy Bell's premises on Forrest Road had a previous life as a grocery shop and, before that, as admin offices for the adjacent poorhouse. Happily, beer, whisky and informal folk sessions long ago replaced thin broth, gruel and oakum-picking shifts.

Formerly known as the Forrest Hill Buffet – and then Bar – its present name stems from a combination of factors: the bar was once owned by the Bell family and one head barman, Alexander (or Sandy) Porter, was known for his enthusiastic ringing of the last orders bell.

From the Scottish folk revival of the fifties to this day, pretty much every notable name in Scottish and Irish traditional music has played here or enjoyed the tunes over a dram or two. Aly Bain, Barbara Dickson, Dick Gaughan, the McCalmans, Phil Cunningham and Dougie McLean are just a few of the Scots.

Back when licensing laws were less liberal, the musicians would finish their last orders and head to a nearby flat owned by the Bells. Safely beyond the jurisdiction of the licensing board, the music would continue in the form of a kitchen ceilidh.

Attempts to modernise have met staunch resistance. The introduction of a fruit machine, TV and jukebox all resulted in the offending items being hauled out onto the street by the regulars. Long-time manager Jimmy Cairney sagely noted that 'Sandy Bell's is full of revolutionaries who want nothing to change'.

Yet Sandy Bell's has evolved. There have been a couple of thoughtful internal renovations and it now even has a coffee machine. That said, it does have just six coffee cups, demonstrating that it remains a boozer at heart.

THE PLAYHOUSE

In its ninety years as a plush pleasure palace, the 3,059-capacity Playhouse has entertained Edinburghers first as a super-cinema and then, following a 'Save the Playhouse' campaign in 1974, as a venue for everything from panto and musicals to punk.

Lou Reed declared the Playhouse his favourite venue in the world and handpicked the theatre for the opening dates of the Velvet Underground's reunion tour in June (1/2) 1993. Not only were these the first shows with founding member John Cale in twenty-five years, they were the influential New York group's first *ever* shows in Europe. (Marking this august occasion, Glasgow band Hugh Reed and the Velvet Underpants took the opportunity to play their own show in a much smaller venue down the road.)

As the UK's largest theatre, the Playhouse has attracted the biggest names in rock, from Queen to Bruce Springsteen to U2, so there was a frisson of expectation in May 1982 when tickets went on sale for a secret show.

Even the venue's staff did not learn the identity of their special guests until the day of the concert, when they were issued with books of blank tickets to be stamped with the artist's name: The Rolling Stones.

While the Playhouse catered for the big guns, the adjacent Nite Club, located on one of the upper floors, became a key hangout for the city's punk and post-punk fraternity in the early eighties, hosting sweaty sets by The Cramps, The Damned, Killing Joke, Bauhaus and The Fall and regular DJ appearances by John Peel.

Homegrown heroes The Fire Engines, Josef K and The Scars represented the local scene and Nite Club alumni U2, Depeche Mode, Eurythmics and Nick Cave all graduated to the Playhouse itself in later years.

Nite Club girls in January 1981. Neither photographer Simon Clegg nor the girls can remember which gig they were at, but they look happy.

Playhouse Theatre
Tuesday 24 Feb. 1981 at 7.30 pm
Stranglers

PLAYHOUSE THEATRE
Greenside Place
Edinburgh

Tuesday 24 Feb. 1981 at 7.30 pm
Doors Open 6.30 pm

STRANGLERS
IN CONCERT
CIRCLE **£3.50**
INC. VAT

Circle £3.50
to be given up

No Ticket Exchanged or Money Refunded—Retain this portion

J 22   J 22

ST CECILIA'S HALL

St Cecilia's Hall, named after the patron saint of music, is the oldest purpose-built concert hall in Scotland and was originally commissioned by the Edinburgh Musical Society as a way of democratising chamber music. When it first opened in 1763, its concerts were so popular that ladies in attendance were politely requested not to 'wear their hoops' or men 'their swords' in order to maximise capacity.

But by the turn of the century, the hall was rendered obsolete as Edinburgh's genteel society took its custom to the newly built Assembly Rooms in the fashionable New Town. The building was subsequently used as a church, Freemasons lodge, school and bookbinder's before housing the Bridge Bar and adjacent Excelsior Ballroom in the mid-twentieth century.

Edinburgh University bought the premises in 1959 to display its collection of historic musical instruments, including a 1766 double-manual harpsichord played by Mozart and such woodwind exotica as the heckelphone and alto fagotto.

Grace Kelly came out of showbiz retirement to do a poetry reading at St Cecilia's for the 1976 Edinburgh International Festival in commemoration of the US bicentenary. Princess Grace was described by the *Scotsman* as 'wrapped in a gown of radiant coral and looking more beautiful than ever'.

In 2008 St Cecilia's received a visit from indie royalty when former Throwing Muses frontwoman Kristin Hersh played an intimate residency, hailed by one onlooker as 'the warmest trauma I've ever been party to'.

The building was revamped and reopened to the public in 2017. Its beautiful oval-shaped Concert Room may be the only place in the world where you can hear eighteenth-century music played on eighteenth-century instruments in an eighteenth-century setting.

THE EDGE FESTIVAL PRESENTS

KRISTIN HERSH
PARADOXICAL UNDRESSING SPOKEN WORD & MUSIC

EDINBURGH ST CECILIAS CHURCH
SUNDAY 17TH - SATURDAY 23RD AUGUST

www.myspace.com/kristinhersh

24HR TICKET HOTLINE: 08444 999 990
ONLINE: WWW.THEEDGEFESTIVAL.COM
IN PERSON: TICKETS SCOTLAND (GLAS & EDIN)
RIPPING (EDINBURGH) GROUCHOS (DUNDEE)

THE**EDGE**FESTIVAL**08**

THE COWGATE: FROM THE CLASH TO COLDPLAY

The Cowgate bars that sit in the shadow of George IV Bridge have long played a vital role in Edinburgh's grassroots music scene. (See Sneaky Pete's entry.) They have also hosted some unexpectedly big names. Bellatrix played the Attic in 1999 and have since vanished without trace. However, their support band, Coldplay, have done all right for themselves.

Other illustrious names include The Clash, who played La Sorbonne, now Subway, in May 1985 as part of their busking tour. Twenty years later, Subway hosted a gig from Arctic Monkeys just before their career went stratospheric.

You just never know who you might see in a late-night dive bar in the Cowgate. In the eighties, Karen Koren's Gilded Balloon venue hosted the likes of Dylan Moran and Craig Ferguson during the Fringe, and famously chucked out Russell Brand for 'abusive behaviour' one night.

To a degree, the Cowgate revels in its louche reputation as one of Edinburgh's more lairy party hot spots. This is not new. From the early 1800s, the second oldest street in the city was known as a 'bedrock of poverty and want' where vagrants and beggars passed their time 'in all kinds of riot and filthy lechery'.

Yet what may be more surprising to the modern reader is that, before that period, in the seventeenth century, the area was renowned as one of the most affluent and fashionable in the city, with lavish mansions and gardens.

One to ponder should you ever find yourself there at chucking-out time on a Bank Holiday Saturday.

THE ROYAL OAK

From Danny Kyle to Karine Polwart, the Royal Oak has long welcomed many of Scotland's more notable folk musicians, and the informal sessions which take place in the bar have a loyal following. Also known as the Grand Ole Opry of Folk, it hosts more structured concerts in the Wee Folk Club in the basement.

You can find the Royal Oak on Infirmary Street, so called because this area was the site of Edinburgh's first hospital. The morgue was situated just below the Royal Oak, and the haunted cellars are said to have been used by the serial killers Burke and Hare to move the bodies of their victims.

EDINBURGH CASTLE

Every August, Edinburgh's most famous landmark supplies the stunning backdrop to the musical and marching spectacular that is the Edinburgh Military Tattoo. The word 'tattoo' comes from the Dutch term 'doe den tap toe', meaning 'turn off the tap' – a last-orders instruction to taverns to ensure soldiers made it back to their barracks at a reasonable hour.

Attracting military bands and performers from as far afield as Indonesia and Samoa, Edinburgh's Tattoo has been attended in its time by over 14 million people and reaches a television audience of 100 million every year. Until the COVID-19 lockdown of 2020 forced the cancellation of all the Edinburgh festivals, the organisers were able to claim that not a single performance had ever been cancelled, come rain or rain.

Pop audiences have also been taking their chances with the weather since 1991, when Van Morrison and Celtic rock titans Runrig kicked off what is now an annual mini season of summer concerts on the Castle Esplanade. Runrig went on to play a record seven Castle Concerts before retiring in 2018. Other previous attractions have included Noel Gallagher's High Flying Birds, Paul Weller, Duran Duran (supported by Florence and the Machine in an apocalyptic downpour) as well as Sir Rod Stewart, Sir Cliff Richard, Sir Tom Jones and Sir Elton John, although a knighthood is not believed to be a prerequisite for performing.

THE QUEEN'S HALL

Edinburgh's Queen's Hall venue in the south side of the city has hosted many memorable musical moments since it was converted from a church to a concert venue in 1979. Opened by the Queen, it typically hosts classical music and artists at the more traditional end of the spectrum, yet it has a proud record of rock and pop gigs by the likes of Nick Cave, David Byrne, Pulp, Calexico and PJ Harvey.

Suede's original guitarist Bernard Butler played his final gig with the band here on 12 February 1994 with a loaf of bread on top of his amp for reasons best known to himself. Ironically, the last song in the set was the band's new single, 'Stay Together'.

SNEAKY PETE'S

In sixties Liverpool, it was the Cavern. In seventies New York, it was CBGBs. We're talking tiny grassroots venues that are disproportionately important to their cities and for the careers of emerging bands. In Edinburgh, it's Sneaky Pete's.

This 100-capacity sweatbox in Edinburgh's Old Town shares the spirit of CBGBs, with its dive-bar vibe and tiny stage. In a former life, it was a pub called Nips o' Brandy and, later, Sneeky Pete's, both known for having the best jukeboxes in the city.

This reputation for carefully curated music continues to this day under the stewardship of Nick Stewart, who took over what was a dodgy vodka bar in 2008 and has gradually developed one of Scotland's most important music spaces.

With club nights and live shows running constantly, it is the heartbeat of Edinburgh's music scene – a vital platform for new talent. Playing a headline show at Sneaky Pete's is, for many local bands, a badge of honour. Young Fathers cite their early gigs here as a crucial step on their journey. When they won the Mercury Music Prize in 2014, it was a surprise to most people – especially the bookies, who had them pegged as outsiders – but not to Stewart, who'd stuck £50 on them to win and landed a tidy £850.

For touring bands, Sneaky's is often the first step into Scotland. Many well-known acts – from Two Door Cinema Club to Ben Howard to Mumford & Sons – have passed through here on their way to bigger things.

DJs love it too; it's perfect for local club nights, and is much loved by big names like Daniel Avery, Erol Alkan and Just Blaze, who return regularly.

In 2019 the club's status was recognised when it won Grassroots Venue of the Year at the Music Week Awards.

Press Club at Sneaky Pete's.

LEITH THEATRE

If there's one venue in Edinburgh that symbolises the city's mix of past glory and huge potential, it's Leith Theatre. Like Edinburgh's music scene, this grand old dame of a building has been through its ups and downs.

Opened in 1932 as Leith Town Hall, it got off to a promising start – but then its main auditorium was damaged by a bomb in 1941. In a sad portent of things to come, it lay dormant for twenty years until it was revived in the sixties by various local organisations and the Edinburgh International Festival.

In the seventies, it came into its own as a live music venue. After a brief name change to the Citadel Theatre, it hosted gigs by Kraftwerk, Thin Lizzy, AC/DC and other big-name touring acts.

Although the theatre was still used by the EIF, the music stopped in the eighties and, by 1988, the building had closed completely.

Sixteen years later, in 2004, with the theatre having fallen into disrepair and on the verge of being sold to property developers, it was rescued by a community group.

In 2017 the building was made habitable by the Hidden Door arts festival and staged gigs for the first time in almost thirty years. Despite Edinburgh lacking live music venues (particularly venues as big as the 1,500-capacity Leith Theatre), many in attendance had never heard of the space before, let alone set foot in it.

The same festival returned in 2018, staging a riotous hometown show by Young Fathers, further showing Leith Theatre's huge potential for Edinburgh's music scene. Kae Tempest, Jarvis Cocker and Neneh Cherry appeared in 2019 as part of the Edinburgh International Festival.

During the COVID pandemic, the Thomas Morton Hall was used as an NHS blood donation venue, a food bank and food poverty charity. You can help protect the future of Leith Theatre by donating here: https://www.justgiving.com/leiththeatretrust.

Inimitable Pulp frontman and solo star Jarvis Cocker returned to the Edinburgh International Festival on 22 August 2019 for a JARV IS show at Leith Theatre.

SUMMERHALL

There can't be many music venues in the world that used to be a dissection room, but welcome to the weird and wonderful world of Summerhall. From 1916 until 2010, this sprawling collection of buildings in Edinburgh's Southside was home to the Royal (Dick) School of Veterinary Studies, or the Dick Vet as it was known locally.

After being taken over by artist Robert McDowell, Summerhall has become an arts hub fizzing with creativity. At its heart is the Dissection Room, a 500-capacity space that has come to play a critical role in Edinburgh's music scene.

Since 2015, a series of gigs under the 'Nothing Ever Happens Here' banner have countered the common complaint that Edinburgh doesn't get its fair share of gigs. From Grandaddy's first Scottish date since reforming as part of Summerhall's fringe programme of 2016, to Pussy Riot and The Dirty Three, the venue has brought hundreds of critically acclaimed artists to the city and provided a showcase for local talent, as well as launching its own Southern Exposure festival and co-producing the new Great Eastern Festival alongside the Queen's Hall and 432 Presents.

THE USHER HALL

When it comes to big gigs in Edinburgh, the Usher Hall is the jewel in the city's crown. Opened in 1914, this grand 5-star concert hall on Lothian Road is to Edinburgh what the Royal Albert Hall is to London – a revered stage for the world's leading musicians.

While the Category A-listed building has a long-established reputation for hosting classical music events, in recent years it has upped the ante, notably following the installation of removable seating in the stalls to allow for standing at contemporary music gigs.

Memorable moments in recent times include Kraftwerk's 3-D concert, Jack White's mobile phone-free show and the intimate, piano-only Conversations with Nick Cave.

THE ROSS BANDSTAND

There aren't many cities in the world where you can see a gig in a garden with a castle perched on top of a dormant volcano as a backdrop – but you can, occasionally, in Edinburgh.

The Ross Bandstand in West Princes Street Gardens dates back to 1877, though the current incarnation was built in the thirties. The open-air theatre beneath the castle has hosted all manner of events since, from VE Day celebrations to Scottish country dancing. It has also hosted occasional concerts, with memorable shows including Garbage who played there in 1999 to mark the opening of the new Scottish Parliament – a big moment not just for the country, but also for Edinburgh-born singer Shirley Manson.

The bandstand has also been used for large-scale electronic music festivals by FLY Open Air, and in 2018, the site became home to the Summer Sessions, an annual event bringing big names such as Kasabian and Lewis Capaldi to the city.

EDINBURGH FESTIVAL THEATRE

There has been a theatre on this Nicolson Street site since 1830, but the current Edinburgh Festival Theatre and its sweeping glass frontage dates to 1994. For thirty years before that, it was known as the Empire Theatre and doubled up as a bingo hall. Any bands playing would have to wait until at least 11 p.m. when the bingo had wrapped up. Presumably Black Sabbath, Elton John, Bowie and The Cramps all had a disco nap in the afternoon before their late night gigs at the Empire.

Fans looking to kill a few hours before showtime could have a drink in the nearby Empire Palace Bar. Or the Rat Trap as it was known to its devotees. Publican Maggie Rae was famous for drying her knickers on the pub's pie machine and chasing customers out of the bar with her 'cudgie stick'. Maggie went on to top a poll of Britain's rudest publicans organised by the *TV-AM* breakfast show in 1984. Having reached this career pinnacle, she retired the next year.

FLY Open Air in Princes Street Gardens.

Plans have been floated to demolish
the current bandstand and replace
it with a new concert venue.

STUDIO 24

Nightclub and Live Music Venue
Open til 3am

CALTON STUDIOS/STUDIO 24

Calton Road, which snakes between the top of Leith Walk and the Palace of Holyroodhouse, was once home to two of Edinburgh's best live music and clubbing venues: the Venue and Calton Studios.

With its fiercely independent ethos, anti-mainstream music programming, bunker-like interior and graffiti-covered exterior, the Calton Studios – later renamed Studio 24 – always felt a bit like an after-party, but one that was happening all the time.

Once a television studio, and then a cinema, it started hosting gigs and clubs in the late seventies and became a home for hard-partying music fans and clubbers all the way through to its last hurrah in 2017. At its best, on any given night, the floor would be a heaving sea of sweaty bodies, tattoos, Day-Glo, leather jackets, lasers, mohicans, dreadlocks, ravers, students and all manner of mavericks from across the city.

In the late eighties and early nineties in particular, it hosted many bands, from the House of Love and Mudhoney to Fugazi and the Smashing Pumpkins. Among its most famous and fondly remembered visitors were Nirvana. They first played in October 1990, the only Scottish show of their tour and a memorable one for which Kurt Cobain personally persuaded one of his favourite bands, the Vaselines, to reform for one night only. They came back on 29 November 1991, just after the release of 'Smells Like Teen Spirit' and a couple of months after *Nevermind* had been released.

Sadly the venue closed in 2017, its owners plagued by constant energy-sapping noise complaints from residents, issues with city council sound restrictions and the looming pressure of property developers.

THE NEW CAVENDISH, COASTERS AND CLOUDS

As Atik, this venue on West Tollcross is best known for its club nights, and superstar DJs such as Calvin Harris have entertained the crowds here. However, it started life in the forties as the New Cavendish, a dancehall whose sprung dancefloor made it ideal for jiving and ballroom dancing.

Along the way, it has been known as the Network, Cav and Lava Ignite, but it was as Clouds, from 1969 to 1979, that it earned a reputation for putting on live bands. Adam and the Ants, Pink Floyd, The Jam and the Ramones all played here.

Edinburgh was very enthusiastic about punk. When the lights went up at the Ramones gig in 1977, even the bouncers were pogoing and a crowd of Edinburgh's early punk pioneers were doing the dying fly – an all-but-forgotten dance that involved lying on your back and pedalling your arms and legs like a bluebottle breathing its last.

In 1979 the venue changed its name to Coasters and, for a while, it operated as a roller disco. Regrettably, history does not record if any rollerblades were ever involved, but bands such as Simple Minds, The Clash, Depeche Mode, Culture Club and R.E.M. also performed here.

HOOCHIE COOCHIE CLUB

The Hoochie Coochie Club, affectionately known as The Hooch, was located above Coasters, and sometimes functioned as that venue's dressing room. In the mid-eighties, it was the hangout for Edinburgh's indie hipsters with early gigs by Primal Scream, The Wedding Present and James. Fred Deakin of electronica duo Lemon Jelly was a student at the time and recalls 'being in awe of Edinburgh's local indie musicians, the legends that I'd only ever seen in the pages of the then-very-Scottish-focused NME, suddenly all around me'. In the late eighties DJ Yogi Haughton played an influential role in the development of dance music culture in Edinburgh with his soul, disco, hip hop and acid house sets (see CLUBBING IN THE CAPITAL).

Rollin', rollin', rollin': Coasters roller disco, where Culture Club toasted their first number one hit 'Do You Really Want To Hurt Me' by showering the front rows with a bottle of Irn-Bru.

THE GAMP AND THE PLACE

These days, the Liquid Room flies the flag for live music on Victoria Street and has hosted gigs by everyone from Moby to Nancy Sinatra. Former venues on this street include the Preservation Halls, the Gamp Club and the Place. The first had a regular roster of blues bands while the Gamp, on Victoria Terrace, was more of a beat or Mod hangout. A Gamp regular fondly recalls the glitterball there, which was most unusual then and considered the height of glamour.

The Place, later the Onion Cellar, was in the basement of the building which, over the years, has been known as Espionage, the Mission, Shady Lady's and Nicky Tam's. The venue was popular with punk bands. At one point, the Place had the dubious honour of being known for having the worst male toilets in town. In fact, we have heard it said that they may have been the inspiration for the Worst Toilet in Scotland scene in *Trainspotting*.

Sticking with matters lavatorial, the loos in the Gamp were behind the stage – potentially embarrassing if you had to pay a visit while a band was playing. On a slightly more wholesome note, there was once a snowball fight between the punters queuing for the Place and the Gampers lining up on the other side of the street. All good, clean fun.

AMERICANA

The Americana Discotheque, one of the largest clubs in Edinburgh in the sixties, was opened by local entrepreneur Paddy Reilly on the site of an old meat market on Fountainbridge, and attracted a lot of out-of-towners.

McGOOS

Edinburgh had a vibrant live music scene for local and touring bands in the sixties. Bungy's Beat Club (on Fleshmarket Close) was a hip coffee-house hangout for the switched-on kids, although one regular remembers that there was so little ventilation, moisture used to drip off the rafters onto your clothes: 'One night, rust spots appeared on the jacket of my new pink moygashel suit. I never went back!'

But McGoos, the former Palace Picture House on the High Street (18–20), seems to have had the edge with their booking policy. It burned briefly but brightly as the favoured hub of Edinburgh's Mod scene in the mid-sixties, running amphetamine-fuelled all-dayers (their licence didn't extend to all-nighters).

One of their flyers claimed 'everyone is going to McGoos because this is where it is all happening' – and with justification. Within a whirlwind two-month period (April–June 1966), McGoos welcomed The Kinks, The Spencer Davis Group, The Small Faces, The Troggs and The Who, with full instrument-trashing shenanigans from Pete Townshend and Keith Moon.

Apparently The Beatles were approached and amenable to appearing, but this modestly proportioned venue was denied a safety certificate to host the world's biggest band. McGoos closed abruptly soon afterwards when, it is alleged, some local gangsters took an overly keen interest in the premises. Rather than cough up protection money, the venue closed – or at least that's the rumour.

TIFFANY'S/CINDERELLA ROCKERFELLAS

Depending on your vintage, there is a space on St Stephen Street, Stockbridge, which will forever be the Pentland Club, Tiffany's or Cinderella Rockerfellas. But this late, lamented club started life as the Grand Theatre, enjoyed a brief canter as a riding academy and then a cinema before becoming one of Edinburgh's most dedicated punk venues.

Flying in the face of convention, Monday nights became the big draw at Tiffany's when a motley assortment of folks who didn't have school in the morning converged under the bizarre fishing-net decor to witness bands such as The Stranglers, Elvis Costello and The Police. The nights were presented by Regular Music (then run by Pete Irvine and Barry Wright), which went on to become one of Scotland's major promoters.

Iggy Pop's show in April 1979 – described by one attendee as 'the real deal' – was interrupted by a bomb scare and the building was evacuated just as the unfettered Iggy got down to his pants. No casualties were reported, though the walls of the neighbouring St Stephen's Church were daubed with Iggy's name.

In stark musical contrast, Tiffany's house band throughout the seventies was the easy-listening ensemble Band of Gold, whose leader Bob Heatlie went on to write Aneka's 'Japanese Boy' and a number of hits for Shakin' Stevens, including hardy perennial 'Merry Christmas Everyone'.

The building was demolished following a fire in 1991.

FLANNIGAN'S

Tucked down Rose Street Lane and promoting itself as 'the TRENDIEST discotheque in the TRENDIEST street', Flannigan's was a much loved soul music hangout – its mission statement posters described it as the place 'where you're never alone' whether 'lover or dancer'. No alcohol was served, but you could buy a coffee and a sausage roll or a Scotch pie – just what you need before hitting the dancefloor. One regular recalls that if the owner liked you, you'd be admitted to 'The Office', a speakeasy where booze was served. Tsk tsk.

THE VENUE

From 'I was there' gigs to seminal club nights, the Venue was the epicentre of Edinburgh's music scene during its hedonistic heyday in the nineties and will forever have a place in the hearts of Edinburgh music fans.

First opened in the early eighties as the Jailhouse, becoming the Venue in 1987, this venue on Calton Road behind Waverley Station was a bastion of alternative music. (Calton Road later became famously associated with the film *Trainspotting*'s opening scene when Ewan McGregor's character, Renton, is nearly hit by a car and gives us his manic grin.)

With its main ground-floor room holding around 400, it was the perfect place for a brilliantly eclectic array of touring bands, including many who would go on to become some of the biggest acts on the planet.

On 11 December 1988, for example, several hundred lucky music fans caught an emerging band from Manchester by the name of the Stone Roses several months before they helped usher in a new era of acid house and youth culture. Likewise, those who bought tickets to see the likes of Suede, the Manic Street Preachers, The Verve and Radiohead in the late eighties and early nineties.

For many, the Venue was about clubbing and, in particular, Pure on Fridays. The incredibly intense weekly dose of Detroit-influenced techno became almost a religion for some (including author Jim Byers) and was one of the world's most revered club nights.

For Chicago house-heads, Tribal Funktion was the highlight of the week, while others got their funk groove on at Chocolate City, run by Jamie Byng, who would later become publisher and MD at Canongate Books.

The Venue closed in 2006, the building having been sold to a property developer. It became an art gallery and, later, offices.

Calton Road, a great location for trainspotting . . . .

Jim Byers' treasured membership card.

PURE ~ EVERY FRIDAY
THE VENUE - CALTON ROAD - EDINBURGH

CAS ROCK

Heads were banged, guitars were thrashed and there were pogos aplenty at this much-missed Edinburgh institution. Opening initially as the Cas Rock Café, it became the Cas Rock – allegedly after objections from a certain Hard Rock Café.

For eight years between 1992 and 2000, it was more than just a pub and live music venue – it was a home away from home for a community of bands and fans with a shared love for punk, rock, metal and indie music.

One of the reasons it was loved so much is that it provided a stage for local bands to cut their teeth. One such act was Idlewild, who honed their live skills there before becoming one of Scotland's most influential and critically acclaimed bands.

Another local act, Annie Christian, bagged a deal with Richard Branson's V2 label the day after playing at one of the bar's annual Planet Pop festivals. Cas Rock also allowed local bands to play regularly, chief among them the likes of the Gin Goblins and the Rab Howat Band, whose shows are the stuff of legend.

The Cas Rock was also a crucial staging post for other Scottish bands making their way up the ladder, with Teenage Fanclub, Mogwai and Snow Patrol all taking to its tiny stage.

From further afield came an array of alternative acts, ranging from the UK Subs and the Meteors to 999, The Fall and Cornershop.

The Cas Rock closed in 2000, with the building becoming a tapas restaurant and, afterwards, a catering equipment shop.

CAFÉ GRAFFITI: LIZZARD LOUNGE

In the mid-nineties, when clubbing and DJ culture was booming, something very special was taking place in the crypt of Mansfield Church at the foot of the city's bohemian Broughton Street. That something was Lizzard Lounge, a self-described 'club night that swam against the tops-off clubbing tide and celebrated live music'.

On Saturday nights, the speakers in the basement space known as Café Graffiti throbbed not to the repetitive beats of house music, but to the polyrhythmic pulse of jazz, soul, blues, hip hop, Afro, Latin and funk.

Founded in 1997 by DJ Joseph Malik, who would later go on to enjoy success as a producer and singer, and multi-talented musician Toby Shippey, Lizzard Lounge brought live music back into the spotlight while at the same time fusing it with DJ sets.

Starting with the house band, the Basic Collective, and DJ sets from Malik, the music and line-ups were exceptionally eclectic, from internationally revered artists such as Donald Byrd and the Blackbyrds and Gil Scott-Heron dishing up R&B, jazz-funk and soul, to live hip hop from local pioneers Blacka'nized or national pioneer Jonzi D. In between, Malik and the team of local DJs (including Ehwun, Unkle Fawaz and DJ Pogo) threw in everything from dub, drum & bass and ska.

Such was its reputation as the coolest club in town that many famous faces popped in, with Björk making a visit in 1997 after her gig at the Usher Hall.

Simon Hodge, of long-running club night Big Beat, joined the team and the club earned a bagful of awards. Sadly, after three glorious years, it all came to an end in December 1999. Café Graffiti had to move out of the church so that repairs could take place. The church is now used for weddings, corporate events and office space.

THE CALEY PICTURE HOUSE

First opened in 1923 as the Caley Picture House cinema, this art deco venue enjoyed two spells as an influential music venue in the capital.

As the Caley Palais in the seventies and eighties, it was a must-visit stop for touring acts such as Mott the Hoople (supported in 1973 by up-and-comers Queen), AC/DC, The Smiths, R.E.M. and New Order.

Following periods as the nightclubs Century 2000 and Revolution, it became the Picture House in 2008 and put Edinburgh back on the map again for gigs, with shows from Mogwai, Wu Tang Clan, The Streets and Basement Jaxx among others.

With a 1,500 capacity, it became a key rung on the city's music venue ladder. Closed in 2013, it reopened as a JD Wetherspoon pub in 2016, and without a mid-size venue, the city has subsequently missed out on a lot of touring acts.

STADIUMS

In 1986, Meadowbank stadium in the east of the city hosted the Commonwealth Games, becoming the first venue in the world to host them twice. But in 1993 something slightly stranger occurred when pint-sized pop star Prince was lowered onstage, in a bed, before belting out a mighty 30-song set. The original stadium, which was demolished in 2019 to be replaced by a new facility, was also used by the T On The Fringe festival for gigs by the likes of the Pixies, Radiohead and Muse.

In other stadium stories, nearby Easter Road, home to Hibernian F.C., once welcomed Elton John onto its hallowed turf, while across town Murrayfield rugby stadium has also hosted its fair share of memorable gigs with visits from U2, David Bowie and Oasis.

Victoria Street, home of beloved music venues, past and present.

PRESERVATION HALL

Named after the legendary New Orleans jazz venue, Edinburgh's Preservation Hall on Victoria Street, affectionately dubbed the Prez, was the stomping ground of the city's blues and rock fraternities, with one regular recalling 'how biker jackets and helmets were taken from you as you went in and put in the cupboard'.

Local legends Tam White and Blues 'n' Trouble played regularly; prestigious guests included Dr Feelgood, Fish and Frankie Miller with Thin Lizzy's Brian Robertson on guitar. Now, it is the Irish bar Finnegan's Wake.

ABC/ODEON

As in many cities, Edinburgh's cinemas doubled as concert venues in the sixties and seventies. The two most rocking picture houses were the ABC and the Odeon – the latter's name an acronym for 'Oscar Deutsch Entertains Our Nation' after the chain's founder.

Elsewhere in this book, you can read about The Beatles' and Bob Dylan's exploits at the ABC and Rollermania at the Odeon on Clerk Street. The Rolling Stones also prowled the ABC stage in May 1964, supporting bouncy beat combo Freddie & the Dreamers, while an unbilled Davie Jones and the Manish Boys opened for Gene Pitney and Gerry & the Pacemakers in December of that year. Their blond moptopped frontman later found fame as a certain David Bowie.

The Odeon's concert heyday was the seventies – alumni include New York icons Richard Hell, Patti Smith and Blondie, hometown heroes The Incredible String Band, and a tardy Lou Reed who was otherwise occupied with a few pre-gig jars in the bar of the Caledonian Hotel.

In June 1979, The Who played one of their first gigs following the death of Keith Moon. That didn't stop fans raising a chant of 'bring back Moonie'. Guitarist Pete Townshend retorted with the withering putdown, 'F**k off, Edinburgh. You're too quiet for The Who.'

PRACTICE ROOMS

In 1968 an early incarnation of the Bay City Rollers played the opening night of the subterranean Caves Club on Blair Street before the space became the Practice Rooms, a rehearsal space for the city's punk and indie bands in the seventies and eighties, including The Exploited, Mike Scott's first band Another Pretty Face and an early incarnation of The Proclaimers, who were nicknamed 'the Buddy Holly skinheads'. Every room was said to have running water – down the walls.

THE WHITE ELEPHANT/VALENTINO'S

The former Palladium variety theatre on East Fountainbridge operated as the White Elephant nightclub in the late sixties and early seventies, selling plates of spam and chips in order to qualify for its late licence as well as hosting the occasional gig by the likes of Slade and local rabble-rousers Writing on the Wall.

Notable for its glistering glam rock interior and bewigged Barbarella-esque go-go dancers (fae Niddrie and Tranent), it was directly attached to the Muscular Arms, whose utterly fabulous acid trip-influenced *American Graffiti* decor was as exotic as that of any London club du jour.

By the turn of the eighties, it was rebranded as Valentino's. According to an Aztec Camera gig review in Dundonian fanzine *Cranked Up*, it 'started off as an over-expensive nosing ground for Edinburgh's spoilt young brats', but its gig list is not to be sniffed at: The Cure, U2, Adam & the Ants and New Order all made early Edinburgh appearances here before larger halls beckoned, while the local post-punk scene was well represented by Josef K, The Ettes, The Delmontes and Boots for Dancing.

THE OASIS CLUB

Located opposite the Festival Theatre in the late sixties, this was another early haunt of the Bay City Rollers when they were fronted by original vocalist Nobby Clark. The Oasis ran an under-16s club on Sunday afternoons – ideal fan fodder for the nascent Rollers. It's now a noodle restaurant.

AQUARIUS/CITRUS CLUB

Hosted gigs by The Associates and Another Pretty Face before finding long life as the Citrus Club. In the early nineties, the Citrus Club hosted the Rhumba Club and other club nights, becoming a key venue for the city's developing house music scene. Now reopened as 4042, a late-night liquor den and ping pong hall.

THE INTERNATIONAL CLUB/FIRE ISLAND

This venue on Princes Street hosted hugely popular Thursday nights in the seventies with local bands such as Café Jacques, before it came into its own in the eighties as beloved gay club Fire Island, run by DJ Bill Grainger. Hailed as one of the top fifty clubs in the world by *The Face*, it was the closest thing Edinburgh had to Studio 54. Eartha Kitt, Divine and the Village People all performed here, and pop mogul Simon Cowell attended on a few occasions to promote his protégé Sinitta.

When Fire Island closed in 1988, the last record played was ABBA's 'Thank You For The Music'. The premises is now an altogether more tranquil branch of Waterstone's.

PALAIS DE DANSE

This fancy Fountainbridge ballroom was frequented by the American Air Force recruits stationed at Kirknewton – who had to meet the approval of a young doorman called 'Big Tam' aka Thomas (later Sean) Connery. Unlike his suited and booted manifestation of James Bond, Connery was well known for breaking bouncer dress code by shedding his bow tie, as well as training for bodybuilding competitions in the ballroom's backstage area.

The venue was famous for its hand-cranked revolving stage, later became a bingo hall, and was eventually demolished to make way for student accommodation.

BUSTER BROWN'S/ELECTRIC CIRCUS

Ronnie McKeown, brother of Bay City Rollers frontman Les, was the resident DJ at archetypal eighties nightclub Buster Brown's, which occupied the site of a former fruit and veg warehouse on Market Street, behind Waverley Station. Hosting aftershow parties for Blondie and Duran Duran, its reputation for glamour persisted through subsequent incarnations as Mercado and Massa, with flyers instructing punters to 'dress up or f★★★ off'.

In 2009 it was reincarnated as the nightclub and live music venue Electric Circus, a much-loved platform for local and touring bands. A young singer from West Lothian called Lewis Capaldi once played the opening slot of a three-band bill, while fellow bright young thing Nina Nesbitt cut her teeth at an open mic night. The venue closed in 2017, and the space has subsequently been developed as an extension of the Fruitmarket Gallery.

STEWART'S BALLROOM/ASTORIA

This dancehall on Abbey Mount hosted northern soul nights and then punk, new wave and reggae shows until the early eighties. Simple Minds were regulars and some lucky people saw Magazine, supported by Bauhaus and Edinburgh's Josef K for £2.50, but the Joy Division booking (for 8 May 1980) was cancelled days before frontman Ian Curtis took his own life.

THE BERKELEY BAR

Located at the bottom of Lothian Road, the Berkeley carved a niche by hosting reggae nights in the early seventies, playing a strict diet of West Indian imports through a jukebox connected to huge speakers.

WIG & PEN

Now well-behaved wine bar Ecco Vino, the bijou Wig & Pen on Cockburn Street hosted early gigs by the likes of Josef K and was a popular punk hangout, not least because the Sex Pistols were said to have supped there on a visit to the city in November 1977. A signing session in Virgin Records was followed by an interview for Radio Forth. DJ Jay Crawford recalled 'they were about two hours late and started carving the table in the studio and they had about twenty or thirty complete tossers following them about'. Their entourage of local fans, including members of post-punk upstarts The Scars, said they felt honoured to be despised by Johnny Rotten.

THE EXCHANGE

This venue near Haymarket Station staged a handful of gigs, most memorably one in 2005 with a young band called Arctic Monkeys. They played here in late 2005, just a few months after they'd appeared at the Subway and a few months before they went stratospheric with the release of their album *Whatever People Say I Am, That's What I'm Not*.

Terminal V

CLUBBING IN THE CAPITAL

Edinburgh has enjoyed a couple of clubbing booms, notably in the 1960s when jazz and blues clubs swung into life and Mod culture grew, and then again in the 1990s as house music swept the nation.

At the peak of club culture in the 1990s, the likes of Glasgow, Manchester, London and Leeds were always name-checked as the leading lights. But Edinburgh had a strong, eclectic and respected scene of its own. That strength continues today, with Edinburgh revered on the international dance music map thanks to the mighty festival-sized events such as FLY and Terminal V. We've picked out a selection of clubs and scenes that were much loved locally and also made waves beyond Edinburgh.

UNIQUE CAPITAL CLUB CURVEBALLS

Edinburgh has always had an artistic sensibility and been a breeding ground for left-field ideas. Three clubs epitomised this spirit in the eighties and nineties – Thunderball, Misery and Going Places – and at their heart was Fred Deakin. With all three, the university arts student and a gang of like-minded creatives started immersive club experiences to a wonderfully eclectic soundtrack.

According to Deakin, his most successful night was Thunderball in the late eighties, which grew from small intimate parties to crowds of 2,000 at the Assembly Rooms. 'We had all sorts of stupid stuff, casinos, bouncy castles, so it was very like a rave except it wasn't acid house all night … It was quite a big deal in Edinburgh at the time, without wanting to blow my own trumpet.'

Deakin's next club hit was Misery, an 'anti-cool club night', which ran in the early nineties, chiefly in The Cooler at the Venue. The music policy – ranging wildly from country & western to rave and soft metal – and marketing was designed to be 'anti-fun'. One infamous flyer simply stated: 'Misery – it's completely shite.' A week after Kurt

Cobain's suicide in April 1994, they presented 'with good taste and impeccable timing' a tribute to Nirvana, with spirits a pound a shot. People loved the irreverence. At one point, the club was featured on Channel 4's *The Word* and it even hit the road for a night at London's Milk Bar.

In the late nineties, Deakin gave Edinburgh an easy listening club, Going Places, in the suitably seventies environs of the ABC cinema on Lothian Road and later a multitude of stylish venues around the city. Driven by Deakin's stylish artwork, Going Places was much loved.

HIDDEN HIP HOP HAPPENINGS

Edinburgh might not be the first city you'd think of when it comes to hip hop. But in fact, the capital was home to a very healthy hip hop scene in the late eighties and nineties. Notable players included Coco and The Bean, MF Outa'National, whose track 'Miles Out of Time' featured on Mo' Wax's 1994 *Headz* compilation, and Blacka'nized, the later incarnation of MF Outa'National, who released tracks on Stereo MCs' label Response. Blackan'ized featured Joseph Malik who would later go on to play a key role in Edinburgh club Lizzard Lounge, sign a solo deal with German label Compost Records, and in recent years, enjoy another creative burst of activity, releasing three albums in three years with UK label Ramrock Red Records. *Diverse Pt. 3* was chosen as a BBC 6 Music Album of the Year in 2021 by presenter Craig Charles. Such was the collective spirit and output of the scene that the fruits of their labour were collected in the 1995 compilation *East Coast Project – A Journey Through the Sound of Edinburgh*.

Club nights Scratch and Seen also played their part in flying the flag for hip hop.

HOUSE MUSIC HEROES

In 1986 northern soul DJ Yogi Haughton, who had moved to Edinburgh from Manchester after falling in love with a local girl, took over the decks at the Hoochie Coochie (see GONE BUT NOT FORGOTTEN) and dished up sets featuring anything from disco and hip hop to acid house and techno.

On the dancefloor, many like Gareth Sommerville were inspired. He began playing hip hop, funk and house at the Kangaroo Klub and went on to to be resident at cult Edinburgh house nights Truth, YIP YAP and Ultragroove. Sommerville was a key figure in the capital's club culture, responsible for bringing a who's who of house DJs to the city.

House music thrived across the city in the nineties. Dogtastic followed a brilliantly eclectic Balearic path, Tribal Funktion got down and dirty to a distinctively Chicago sound, while Burger Queen took a much more irreverent approach, injecting a sense of fun and glamour to Saturday nights.

For harder house sounds, two clubs ruled the city: Joy, the much loved gay night, and Taste, the decadent Sunday nighter aimed at 'Extroverts and Perverts'. For those who favoured progressive house and trance, Sublime created a night, sound and community that burned brightly.

No story of clubbing in Edinburgh is complete without mention of Pure. Running at the Venue (see GONE BUT NOT FORGOTTEN) for a decade in the nineties, led by DJs Twitch and Brainstorm, it began with eclectic electronic sounds, breakbeats and deep house.

Gradually, the dark, smoke-filled sweaty dancefloor pulsed to a Detroit-leaning techno sound, courtesy of guests like Jeff Mills and Derrick May, and a hard acid edge.

Its members developed an almost religious devotion to this Friday night which attracted a memorably diverse congregation of clubbers of all ages and from all walks of life.

CONTEMPORARY CLUB GIANTS

Today's clubbers in Edinburgh are spoilt for choice, with two world-class electronic music events on their doorstep.

Built on the foundations of its weekly FLY Club night and other parties around the city (and beyond), FLY Open Air Festival is held twice a year. Its exuberant events feature the biggest names in the DJ world in spectacular locations such as Princes Street Gardens beneath Edinburgh Castle and the grounds of stately home Hopetoun House.

With a slightly harder edge, Terminal V takes place at Easter and Halloween at the Royal Highland Centre, Ingliston, a venue capable of attracting a remarkable 40,000 over two days.

Both events feature huge production levels, line-ups and audiences – in a way that hasn't been since the early nineties Rezerection raves at the Royal Highland Centre.

DRUM AND BASS IN THE PLACE

One word: Manga. For a dozen years, Edinburgh clubbers of a jungle and drum and bass persuasion found their home at this institution of break beats. Driven by founder George Macdonald, aka G-Mac, and resident DJ Kid, the club enjoyed a halcyon period at La Belle Angele, with shows from scene leaders such as DJ Hype and Roni Size and a live broadcast on BBC Radio 1, before the venue was sadly reduced to ruins by a fire.

DJ Kid, left, and G-Mac, right, at Manga.

MOVERS AND SHAKERS

There isn't room to namecheck everyone and everything musical we like in Edinburgh, but here's a selection of our favourites.

Dot Allison, musician
Assembly Rooms, venue
Athens of The North, label
Avalanche, independent music shop
Bannermans, venue
Blanck Mass, artist
Bongo Club, venue
Broken Records, band
Captain's Bar, pub
The Caves, venue
Check Masses, band
Callum Easter, artist
Edinburgh Folk Club
Edinburgh Jazz and Blues Festival
Edinburgh Gig Archive, website
EH FM, radio station
Elvis Shakespeare, records and books
Finitribe/Finiflex, band and label
Firecracker, label
Fopp, record shop
Vic Galloway, BBC Radio Scotland
Gerry Loves Records, DIY record label
Greentrax, traditional music recording company
Henry's Cellar Bar, venue
Idlewild, band

La Belle Angele, venue

Lau, folk band

Neil Landstrumm, artist

Leith Depot, venue

Maranta, band

The Mash House, venue

MC LOTOS, rapper

Meursault, band

The Nectarine No 9, indie band

Neu! Reekie!, literary collective and cross-culture curators

O2 Academy Edinburgh, venue

Paradise Palms, bar, record shop and label

Proc Fiskal, artist

Scottish Post-Punk, Facebook and Twitter

Song By Toad, record label

Stanley Odd, band

Stereogram Recordings, independent record label

Thorne Records, record shop

Wee Red Bar, venue

We Were Promised Jetpacks, band

Voodoo Rooms, venue

Wide Days, music convention

Siobhan Wilson, singer-songwriter

Withered Hand, musician

EPILOGUE

At the time of writing in early 2022, live music is firing up once again in the bars and venues of Edinburgh. The COVID-19 pandemic has tested the ingenuity of the city's musicians, record labels and gig promoters, who responded with online shows, a wealth of new recorded music and socially distanced pop-up venues.

Despite concerns for the sustainability of the city's music venues in the long-term, there have been positive developments in the live scene. The under-used and under-loved Corn Exchange venue in Slateford has been rebranded as the O2 Academy Edinburgh, joining an established portfolio of mid-sized venues which form a tight touring circuit round the UK, and bolstering the chances of attracting more international acts to the city.

Plans for the building of Edinburgh's first new concert hall in over a century have been given the green light, following the resolution of a protracted disagreement with the developers of the neighbouring St James Quarter. The 1,000-capacity Dunard Centre, to be located behind Dundas House on St Andrew's Square and slated for completion in 2025, will provide a permanent home for the Scottish Chamber Orchestra and be used as a principal venue for the Edinburgh International Festival as well as hosting rock, pop and jazz shows year-round.

The big plans don't end there. Plans for an 8,000-seat indoor arena in Straiton were tabled in late 2019, while proposals for a national music centre sited in the Old Royal High School on Calton Hill have been endorsed by Edinburgh City Council, with £55 million in funding pledged by the backers of the Dunard Centre. The fate of this iconic neoclassical building is a long-rumbling saga but this is an encouraging step towards realising its future use as a music school, concert venue and visitor centre.

Meanwhile, back at street level, Edinburgh has spawned a fresh generation of exciting musicians, including singer-songwriter Bonnie Kemplay who saw off 10,000 fellow competitors to win the first ever Radio 1 Live Lounge Introducing award and pop singer Bow Anderson who has made a streaming splash with her first singles.

Other bright lights include Edinburgh-born Scots-Chinese electronica artist LVRA, winner of the Sound of Young Scotland Award at the Scottish Album of the Year (SAY) Awards in 2021, and rapper Nova, who won the 2020 SAY Award for her debut *Re-Up*.

The likes of Swim School, Retro Video Club and Vistas keep the indie fires burning and idiosyncratic performers Hamish Hawk and Callum Easter take a leaf out of the Rezillos' playbook by sounding like no one else but themselves.

All are reasons to be cheerful about the next round of Edinburgh's greatest hits.

SOURCES AND ACKNOWLEDGEMENTS

We particularly want to acknowledge the following: Alan Edwards and Simon Clegg for their photographs; *Howff tae Hip Hop* by David Irving (2013); *All That Ever Mattered: The History of Scottish Rock and Pop* by Brian Hogg (2001); the Lost Edinburgh Facebook page; the Edinburgh Gig Archive; Scottish Post-Punk; and edinphoto.org.uk.

Thanks go to Ian Rankin for his foreword, Kathryn Haldane for the venue and location photography, Ken McNab for Beatles stuff and editor Alison Rae for the tickets and record covers.

PHOTOGRAPHY CREDITS

Leith Theatre courtesy of Gaelle Beri
Elvis Shakespeare photograph courtesy of Alison Rae
Vinyl Villains © Shutterstock
Jackie Dennis © Pictorial Press Ltd/Alamy
Hamish Henderson © Ketzel Henderson/Sandy Paton/SSS Archive
The McKinleys © Pictorial Press Ltd/Alamy
Bay City Rollers © Trinity Mirror/Mirrorpix/Alamy
Shirley Manson © TheCoverVersion/Alamy
The Waterboys © Barry Cronin/Alamy
The Rezillos © Records/Alamy
The Proclaimers © Pictorial Press Ltd/Alamy
Nirvana at the Southern Bar courtesy of Alan Edwards
Beatles fans at the ABC cinema © Trinity Mirror/Mirrorpix/Alamy
Harmonica © Shutterstock
Green Day poster courtesy of Colvin Cruickshank
Clash ticket courtesy of Colin McNeill
David Bowie © Keystone Press/Alamy
The Beta Band courtesy of John Maclean/Vic Galloway
Dizzy Gillespie © Trinity Mirror/Mirrorpix/Alamy
The Exploited © Janine Wiedel/Photolibrary/Alamy
Vicky Leandros © Keystone Press/Alamy
Judge Dread © Pictorial Press Ltd/Alamy
Bruce's Records courtesy of Simon Clegg/Mike O'Connor
Nite Club girls courtesy of Simon Clegg/Mike O'Connor
Sneaky Pete's courtesy of Nick Stewart
Jarvis Cocker © Iain Masterton/Alamy
Ross Bandstand © Shutterstock
FLY Open Air courtesy of FLY

Studio 24 wall © Alan Wilson/Alamy
Coasters courtesy of Simon Clegg/Mike O'Connor
Terminal V courtesy of Hannah Metcalfe
Record boxes © Shutterstock
Leith graffiti courtesy of Catriona Campbell
Edinburgh Music Tours © Jannica Honey
Colin Stetson © James Duncan

Spotted in locked-down Leith, April 2021.

A NOTE ON THE AUTHORS

JIM BYERS runs Edinburgh Music Lovers (EML), a platform and occasional promoter of special events for a community of like-minded music fans. He started his career as a music journalist, first in Edinburgh and later in London, before moving into PR and communications. Aside from EML, Jim is director of the Beeline PR agency.

FIONA SHEPHERD is an established music journalist who has been attending gigs and writing about the music scene since 1990. She is the chief rock and pop critic for the *Scotsman*, and also writes for *Scotland on Sunday*, *The List* and *Edinburgh Festivals* magazine.

ALISON STROAK has been a bookseller, publisher and editor. Alison managed the legendary John Smith's Bookshop on Byres Road when it was one of the favourite haunts of Glasgow's music fraternity. (It was also during this time that she suggested to playwright/director Harry Gibson that *Trainspotting* might make a good play . . .)

JONATHAN TREW has been writing about music, culture and restaurants since the early nineties. A brief stint as a music reporter for MTV convinced him he was more useful as a keyboard jockey than in front of a camera.

Jonathan, Fiona and Alison are co-founders/directors of Glasgow Music City Tours and Edinburgh Music Tours, which offer guided music-themed walking tours that explore the rich musical history of both cities.

EDINBURGH MUSIC LOVERS

Founded by Jim Byers (pictured above), EML is a platform providing carefully curated content and eclectic events and experiences for a community of discerning music fans in Edinburgh. Previous EML events and special projects have featured guests such as Colin Stetson (pictured below), Kojey Radical, Erland Cooper, Swim School, The Howl & The Hum, Arlo Parks, and The Love Frequency, an exploration of music's impact on wellbeing featuring Felix Buxton from Basement Jaxx and a choir.

Find out more at Edinburghmusiclovers.com and @weareEML.

EDINBURGH MUSIC TOURS

Hear the story of the musicians who have stayed, played and made music in Scotland's capital city with these entertaining, guided walking tours.

Private tours in Edinburgh are available on request. Glasgow tours are scheduled for April to September. For more information, see: www.glasgowmusiccitytours.com.

Contact us on info@glasgowmusiccitytours.com.